Our New Home on the Hill
A Promise from Papa
Friedrich Guenther

To anyone who finds my journal:

All the able men in our village have left to fight in the War Between the States. So we women and children must protect ourselves from vigilantes and hostile Indians here on the Texas frontier.

I cannot know how this journal will end, whether Papa and Eduard, my true love, will come home. I can only strive to keep my family safe until they do.

Anna Sophie Franziska Guenther

Village Without Men

Sophie's Second Journal

Janice Shefelman

Cover Painting by
Karl Shefelman

Illustrations by
Judy Ireson

EAKIN PRESS Fort Worth, Texas
www.EakinPress.com

A glossary of German and Spanish words can be found on pages 185 - 187.

Published By Eakin Press
An Imprint of Wild Horse Media Group
P.O. Box 331779
Fort Worth, Texas 76163
1-817-344-7036
www.EakinPress.com

1 2 3 4 5 6 7 8 9
Paperback ISBN 978-1-68179-226-2
Hardback ISBN 978-1-68179-262-0
eBook ISBN 978-1-68179-260-6

Comfort, Texas

Tuesday
April 12, 1864

Dear Reader,

What is to become of us — of me, Sophie?

This War Between the States began on my twelfth birthday. Today I turned fifteen, and the war turned three. Thousands of men have died fighting to decide if we are one country or two. Will it ever end?

Tonight I sit at our wood plank table before the fire, writing these words in my new journal. Papa sent it for my birthday and drew the picture of a new house he will build for us when he returns. For now, we live in a one-room cabin behind the Bremers' home on High Street because after Papa left to join the Union Army, vigilantes burned our house to the ground. We were lucky to get out alive and to have friends like *Frau* Bremer. Of course, Comfort is a small village and people help each other, especially in times of trouble.

Mama and my little brother Willie and sister Lena are asleep at the other end of the room. A folding screen separates us. It has been raining in torrents all day, but rain is not the worst thing that happened.

After school today *Tante* Emma gave a birthday party for me at her house. She is not really my aunt, just a family friend. Her five young children, along with Willie and Lena, were eating birthday cake at the round dining table.

I wore my best blue floral dress with a lace collar. A seamstress in Comfort made it out of cotton fabric Mama had kept for a long time. We get very little cloth now that our Gulf ports are blockaded.

Mama and *Tante* sat on either side of the fire in wing chairs while my redheaded friend Etta and I settled on the soft velvet couch, although settled is not a good description of her. She never seems to sit still and consumed her cake in no time, a Black Forest chocolate cake topped with cherries and whipped cream.

"Oh, *Frau* Altgelt, this is the best cake I ever tasted!" Etta said.

"*Ja,* it may be the last of the chocolate and cherries until President Lincoln lifts his Gulf blockade." *Tante* nodded toward the kitchen. "You must tell my mother how much you liked it, Etta, for I can take no credit. I have never even boiled an egg, nor do I care to."

"Were you a *Wildfang* as a girl, like me?"

Tante smiled. "I still am, Etta. I prefer riding out to look for our cattle with my husband — when he was here — while my *liebe* mother does the cooking for us."

Probably that is why she is still slim, even after having five children. I like her independent attitude. I am no *Wildfang* but I am determined to think for myself.

As we talked, raindrops slashed against the windows but we were cozy and comfortable until ... there came a loud knocking on the front door.

"Himmel!" Tante Emma frowned. "Only trouble would come knocking on such a day." She set her plate aside and rose hesitantly, looking toward the door.

Was it vigilantes? I shuddered, remembering the night when some men came to our door and threatened to hang

Papa if he didn't join the Confederate Army. Rebel Rabble, I call those men.

The rustling of *Tante*'s long skirts brought me back to the present. We all sat breathless as she stepped to a bookcase, unlocked the foldout desk, and took out a revolver.

"No fighting!" Willie yelled and ran to me.

I hugged him close while Mama took Lena on her lap.

"Don't open the door, Emma," Mama said.

Tante looked at her for a moment. "If it's some of those vigilantes, they will knock it down anyway, Elisabet."

Frau Murck, *Tante*'s mother, came out of the kitchen, sat down at the table, and pulled her two youngest grandchildren onto her lap. "Stay here, *meine Lieben,* and be quiet."

Etta clutched my arm. For once she was speechless. We all waited in tense silence.

Tante cocked the revolver, opened the door, and took her stance. With arms outstretched she held the gun in both hands.

A group of men with handkerchiefs tied over their lower faces stood outside on the front gallery.

"I'll shoot the first man who comes through the door."

I thrilled at her bravery.

A small man in the center with heavy black eyebrows and mean eyes said, "Lady, we're lookin' for one of them bushwhackers, name of Sam Fisher. Thought he might be hidin' around here somewheres."

Without lowering the revolver, *Tante* said, "And who might you be?"

He pulled his bandanna down, revealing a bushy mustache. "The name is Waldrip and these here men are my

Wolfpack. Waldrip's Wolfpack. Kinda has a nice sound, don't it?"

Biting her lips together, *Tante* did not answer but kept her eyes and gun on him.

"You might of heard about us, the *Hängerbande* you Germans call us. We don't hang women, only men who ain't fightin' for the Confederacy, men who run and hide in the bushes. You seen one of them around here, lady?"

She shook her head. "No, now leave us before my trigger finger twitches."

"No fighting," Willie said.

So true, I thought. Willie says this whenever people argue, like when Papa and Mama used to argue over living here in the "wilderness," as she calls it.

The men chuckled, and Waldrip looked at Willie, who turned away and buried his face against my side.

"Sure thing, kid, after we have a look around."

"Not in my house!" *Tante* Emma said.

Waldrip surveyed the room with its velvet curtains, upholstered chairs from New Orleans, the china and silverware on the table. *Tante* had one of the most refined homes in the village due to *Herr* Altgelt's family wealth.

"Mighty nice place you got here, lady. I'd sure hate to see it go up in flames some night."

I heard Etta gasp. Remembering how that very thing happened to our house a year ago, I said, "*Tante,* let him look. You have nothing to hide."

Silence. Rain pounded on the gallery roof, and chilly air blew in through the door as she considered.

Finally she said, "Very well, but only you, Mister Waldrip, only you. And take off your boots. I'll keep my gun on your Wolfpack while you search."

He chuckled as if he did not believe that such a pretty woman would have the nerve to actually shoot, even though she had a steely eye. I knew she would and that she was a good shot. Not long ago she and I had a target practice down in a ravine of Cypress Creek. We shot at a small rock on the other side. I watched her point, aim, slowly squeeze the trigger, and shatter it.

Waldrip removed his boots and stepped in, scowling at us. We sat like statues, only moving our heads to follow him. His black coat dripped water as he disappeared through the kitchen door.

Etta whispered, "He scares me."

I nodded.

"Me, too, Sophie," Willie said, looking up at me.

"They could ravish us," Etta added. "They all have guns and we only have one."

I shushed her but Willie heard. "What's ravish? Are they going to shoot us?"

I caught my breath. "No, Willie, no one is going to hurt you, I promise." I only hoped I could keep my promise.

It was true that they could overpower *Tante* and take her gun. Oh, if only Papa were here.

After slamming cabinet doors in the kitchen, Waldrip moved on to *Tante*'s bedroom. More slamming of wardrobe doors. Then he returned to the living room and stomped upstairs to the children's bedrooms. Three-year-old Helene escaped from her grandmother's arms, ran to her mother, and clung to her skirts, wailing. Some of the other Altgelt children started crying, but *Tante* ignored them and kept her eyes fixed on the Wolfpack.

Willie stayed quiet, as did Lena, who snuggled in Mama's arms. "*Guter* boy," I whispered into his ear.

He looked over at Lena. "*Gute* girl." I could not help smiling.

Waldrip came downstairs. "Shut those kids up."

"When you leave, they will stop," *Tante* said.

"I'm leavin', lady, but we're gonna look around outside in the bushes and smokehouse." He jerked on his boots. "Sooner or later we'll find that traitor."

As soon as he stepped out on the gallery, *Tante* shut the door, turned the lock, and looked over at her children. "Hush now, *Kinder,* enough crying." Slowly, occasionally sniffing, they quieted as *Frau* Murck comforted them.

Then with little Helene tagging along on her skirts, *Tante* placed the revolver back in the desk and locked it. She sent the child to her grandmother and turned to us, her face drained of color.

Mama said, "Oh Emma, you were so brave!"

"Well, Elisabet, that comes from being a soldier's daughter back in Germany." She shook her head. "But at times like this I wish I lived in San Antonio."

"Or Dresden," Mama added.

I understood her desire to return to safety in Dresden near her parents. Both pairs of my grandparents lived there, and sometimes I wished for the same. But I also knew that Papa could never go back to Dresden. He would be put in prison or worse for joining the street demonstrations in rebellion against King Frederick. The revolt failed and many of the demonstrators were arrested or fled Germany. Papa and Mama fled to France with their baby daughter — me. From there we sailed to Texas.

Tante took a deep breath and sighed. "*Ja,* Elisabet, but we are here now and have to make the best of it we can — you without your Friedrich and me without my dashing cavalier."

That is what *Tante* calls her husband, Ernst Altgelt. He returned to Germany to care for his ailing father at his wife's urging. But I think he simply did not want to fight in the war on either side. Who could blame him?

"Sophie," she went on, "I must say that your birthdays seem to attract unusual visitors."

It was true. When I turned thirteen, a friendly Comanche chief of the Penateka band visited us. His name is Tsena and Papa made a painting of him. I will never forget him because later he helped save Papa's life.

Etta sat up straight, flipped her red braids over her shoulders, and said, "*Ja*, I was there too. It was scary — at first."

"But not as much as this time," I said.

"Well, now let us forget those ruffians and continue with our party," *Tante* said. "*Kinder*, there is more cake, and Sophie, I think your mother has a surprise."

Willie detached himself from me and ran to the table with the Altgelt children.

Lena shook her head no, no cake, and clung to Mama.

Standing, Mama put Lena on the couch beside me and I cuddled her. After stepping into *Tante's* bedroom, Mama returned with a book in hand.

"For you, Sophie, from your papa, sent all the way from New York."

I gasped. A new journal, bound in blue leather with gold tooling around the edges. I clasped it to my heart. It was surprising that any mail got through the blockade. Only a few blockade runners managed to sneak into Galveston and smaller ports, bringing us supplies, newspapers, mail, and now my journal. Still, we suffered shortages of coffee, salt, flour, even clothing and shoes.

I looked up at Mama and smiled. She has blonde hair braided and wrapped around her head like a halo. No one would think we are mother and daughter, for my hair is dark and curly like Papa's. And he and I have a widow's peak and dimples. We are alike in other ways too. We both like to read and question the way things are. Questions like why do men kill each other in war? And what is *Gott?* Papa is a Freethinker and so am I.

"Papa surely knows what I like. If only he were here."

"If he were, he would be in trouble," said *Tante,* "so be careful what you wish."

I nodded. It was the sad truth. Waldrip would consider Papa a traitor for refusing to fight for the South. We Germans in Comfort live on an island surrounded by a sea of rebels.

Mama picked up Lena and sat down again.

Willie came running. "What is it, Sophie?"

"Open it, Sophie, open it!" Etta said, bouncing up and down on the couch.

There was a letter folded inside the cover. I read it aloud and will paste it here:

New York
March 13, 1864

To my *liebe* Sophie —

I can hardly believe you will soon be fifteen years old! Or that I have missed two years of your life Hopefully the war will soon be over, and I can come home before your next birthday.

Yours,
Papa

"Oh, I hope so!" I said.

Willie pointed to a drawing on the first page. "Look, Papa drew a house for you."

"*Ja*, a rock house, not a cabin," I told Willie. "He says this is the house he'll build for us when he comes home."

As you might have guessed, dear Reader, my papa is an artist. He used to draw political cartoons for the *San Antonio Zeitung* that criticized the Confederacy and got him in trouble.

"When is he coming home?" Willie asked.

"When the war is over."

"When will it be over?"

"Soon." But of course no one knew, and I don't think Willie was convinced.

If only Papa could have gone back to Germany like *Herr* Altgelt. Instead he joined a group of Comfort men, including Eduard, headed for Mexico and thence to New York to join the Union Army. Confederates followed them and made a surprise attack on the Nueces River. Papa was wounded in the leg. No one knew what happened to Eduard. When we got word, I rode out there and brought Papa home but as soon as his leg healed he left again.

After weeks of anxious waiting, we received a letter from him saying not only that he had safely crossed the Rio Grande into Mexico, but also that he met up with Eduard. Together they were taking passage to New York. I received a letter from Eduard too, promising that one day we would see each other again.

I wish I could be sure. But in times of war *nothing* is sure.

Months later we learned that they had arrived in

New York. Since his leg made him unfit to join the army, Papa got a job doing battle drawings for *Harper's Weekly*. Though he has to go to the battle sites, I hope soldiers don't kill artists.

He was sent to the Battle of Gettysburg last summer and was there on the third and last day. We received a letter from him saying that he sat on a rock outcropping behind the Union lines and saw the Confederate soldiers mowed down as they approached across an open field.

Eduard enlisted and was dispatched for training. Since then I have received occasional letters from him but I suspect some did not make it through the blockade, just as my letters to him. He was assigned to the Union Army of Tennessee. I shudder to think of him fighting in battles. And knowing this, he does not write to me about it.

Now I must bank the fire and climb into my own bed, not the lovely bed with carved wings on the head and footboards. No, it was a victim of the fire that destroyed our house, along with Papa's paintings, Mama's piano, and our books.

Even so, I am thankful to have a warm cabin and a bed, especially on a cold, rainy night like this. I have always loved listening to the rain as I fall asleep. Still, I cannot help worrying about what tomorrow will bring to our little village without men.

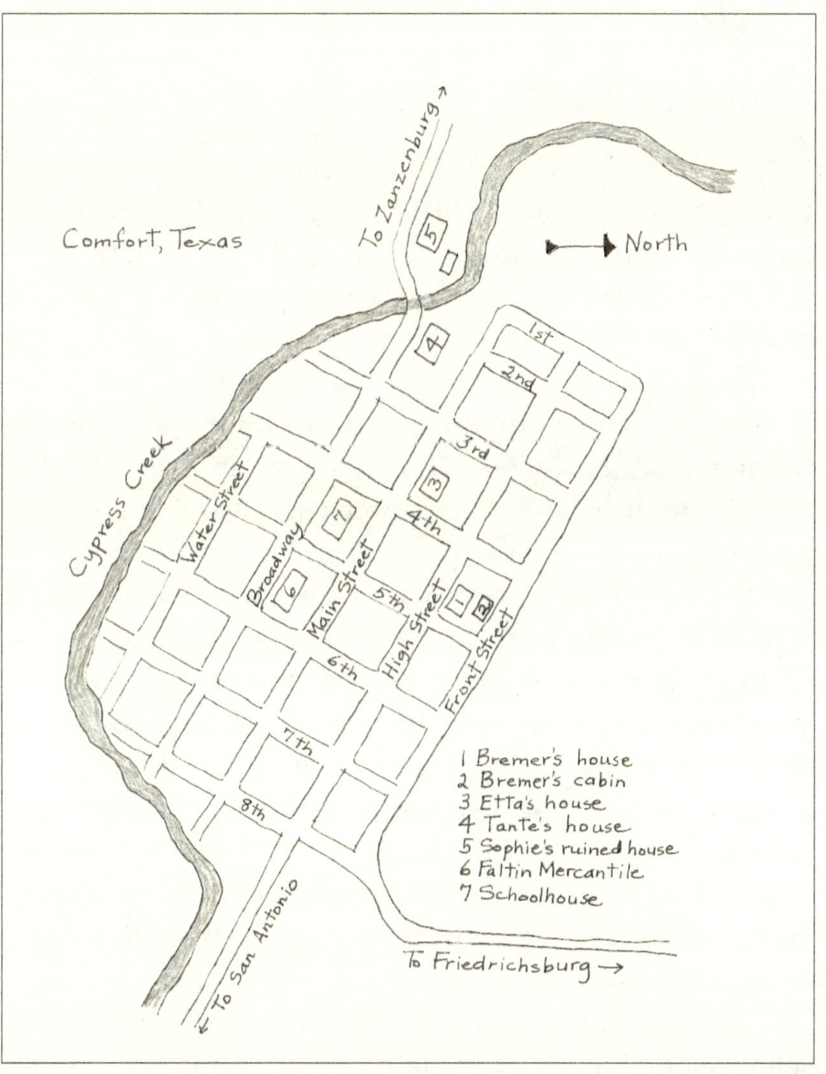

Comfort, Texas
North
To Zanzenburg
Cypress Creek
1st
2nd
3rd
4th
5th
6th
7th
8th
Water Street
Broadway
Main Street
High Street
Front Street
To San Antonio
To Friedrichsburg
1 Bremer's house
2 Bremer's cabin
3 Etta's house
4 Tante's house
5 Sophie's ruined house
6 Faltin Mercantile
7 Schoolhouse

Friday
April 15, 1864

To help you imagine our little village, dear Reader, I have drawn a map of Comfort. Papa could do a better job, but my map will have to do, for who knows when he will return.

Some of the houses are log cabins, chinked with stone and mortar, some are stone and half timbers, which we Germans call *Fachwerk*. The only store in town is Faltin Mercantile. It looks like our houses, only wider. The log schoolhouse is on Broadway, a street that is not at all like the Broadway in New York City. I have heard that it is lined with four- and five-story buildings.

Since our teacher, *Herr* Steves, had to leave because of the war, *Tante* took over his job. She always wanted to be a teacher, and three of her five young children needed lessons. Rather than use the schoolhouse, she set up a school in her home, invited all the children in Comfort, and asked Etta and me to be her assistants. I teach seven little ones, including Willie, to read using McGuffey Readers. Etta teaches them sums.

This morning after breakfast Willie and I set out for school along 5th Street to Main and down to Etta's house. She was waiting for us on the front gallery.

"*Guten Morgen,* Sophie, and *kleiner* Willie," she said, leaping down the steps.

"I'm not little," Willie said, pulling himself up straight. "Only my papa can call me that."

"Ach, sorry. How about sweet Willie?"

He sighed. "Just Willie, *bitte,"* please.

Sometimes Etta can be annoying. "Leave him be," I said. "He misses his papa."

"Well, so do I, but they will come back, Willie."

"How do you know?"

"I don't but I hope."

The sun was shining in a clear blue sky, and a soft breeze stirred. A few other children, some with their mothers, walked along Main Street toward *Tante*'s house. Near the edge of town bluebonnets and Indian paintbrush filled a meadow that sloped down to Cypress Creek.

"Let's pick some flowers for *Tante,"* Willie said as he wandered into the meadow.

After he picked a handful, we walked on to her house. Children gathered on the front gallery, waiting for *Tante* to open the door and ring the school bell.

When she did, Willie stepped up and handed her the bouquet clutched in his fist.

"Danke, Willie." Thanks. "What a little gentleman."

I saw Willie open his mouth to protest *little.*

"Willie, a gentleman replies, My pleasure."

He glanced at me, smiled, and nodded his head. "My pleasure, *Tante."* There never was a sweeter boy.

After *Tante* told us to take our places, my reading group gathered at the round dinner table.

"Let's open our books to Lesson XIII," I instructed them.

There were ten new words in this lesson and a picture of a boy with his dog.

"This dog looks kind of like Max." Willie looked up at me with his sad blue eyes.

I felt a pang of grief. Max, our loyal sheepdog who died protecting us from vigilantes. My voice thickened. *"Ja,* he does."

Willie stood and wrapped his arms around my neck. "Don't be sad, Sophie. He lives in our hearts, like you said."

"*Danke*, Willie. You are right."

"I remember Max," *Tante*'s George said.

"What happened to him?" one of the other children asked.

"He barked until those mean men shot him," Willie said.

Silence. All the children looked to me to make sense of such evil. For a moment I did not know what to say but Willie had an idea.

Brightening, he said, "Let's pretend this dog is Max."

I nodded. "Good idea."

After we sounded out the list of new words, I asked Willie to read the first sentence.

"Look – at – Tom – and – his – dog ... Max."

"Good, now you, George."

"The – dog – has – a - black – spot – on – his – back."

"Good."

Then I called on little curly haired Julia.

She smiled and read, "Do – you – think – he - is – a – good – dog?"

"JA!" YES! the children shouted.

Tante's group of older students turned to look at us.

"Kinder!" Children! "Not so loud, *bitte," Tante* said.

My group giggled.

Etta was sitting at the foldout desk reading a tan leather-bound copy of Homer's *Odyssey* with its gilt title on the spine. *Tante* had assigned us to take turns with the book.

"Oh, *Frau* Altgelt, may I join Sophie's group? They are having more fun. I cannot understand this story. It's so ancient."

"Just keep on trying, Etta, and we will discuss the story later while the little ones rest. I have assigned it for a reason."

Etta sighed and did so.

Unlike Etta, I could not wait to continue reading the book. I had read *The Iliad* and wondered if Odysseus would ever manage to get home after the Greeks conquered Troy. He survived the war but on his journey home he and his seamen faced many perils and angered Poseidon, god of the sea.

I like the idea that gods and goddesses helped or hindered events. The goddess Athena favored Odysseus because he used his intelligence to overcome disaster. Maybe I should pray to her to protect Papa and Eduard and bring them safely home.

After we had lunch and the little ones lay down on the floor to nap, *Tante,* Etta, and I sat around the dining table to talk about *The Odyssey.*

"Etta," *Tante* said, "Why do you think I have asked you to read *The Odyssey?*"

"Because you hate me?" Etta said and grinned.

Tante and I laughed. *"Nein, meine Liebe,"* she went on. "There are two reasons. One, Greek myths and stories are the foundation of our culture. And since most of us who settled Comfort were educated in German universities, we want our children to be well educated too."

She turned to me. "And what do you think the other reason is, Sophie?"

"I think because we are all wondering if our men will survive the war and return, just like the Greek women."

"*Ja,* Sophie, you read my mind."

"Well then, don't laugh, but I was just wondering if we should pray to Athena."

Etta looked at me as if I were crazy, but she did not laugh. "Are you serious, Sophie?"

"*Ja,* we're Freethinkers, are we not? Papa always said we're free to think for ourselves about God ... and goddesses."

Tante smiled. "Indeed we are, and thanks to my dashing cavalier, we have a community of Freethinkers."

It was true. *Herr* Altgelt organized this settlement in Comfort, and our family joined him.

"So, *meine Lieben,* let us pray to the goddess. Sophie, go ahead."

Etta gave me a smirk. I ignored it and gathered my thoughts for a moment.

"Athena, goddess of wisdom and daughter of Zeus, hear me. Keep our men safe in battle and bring them home to us."

"*Sehr gut,* Sophie." Very good. "Now, I'm assuming you have both finished reading Book Five. Am I correct?"

"*Ja,*" Etta and I said in unison.

"So, to begin let's talk about Queen Penelope, loving wife of Odysseus. What do you think of her as a woman? She has been waiting for her husband to come home from the war for ten years. Meanwhile, a hundred suitors not only court her, they have installed themselves in the palace, drinking the Queen's wine and devouring her food.

But she will not choose from among them because she hopes her husband will return."

Etta stood, put her hands on her hips, and kicked the air. "I think she should kick them out. Where's her backbone?"

Tante and I chuckled.

"I agree," I said, "but I admire her faithfulness to her husband."

Tante smoothed a loose strand of dark hair into the bun atop her head. "You may know that Greek women had little power over their fates, even less than modern women. They needed a man to secure their rights. Thus, Penelope worries that her husband might never return, and she is cunning enough to know that if not, she would need to marry another."

"Still, I think she only loves him," I said.

Tante nodded. "So, now for our hero, Odysseus. He struggles on and on to return home. What do you think of him as a man?"

"He is noble and loves his wife and son and homeland," I said. "No matter what obstacles Poseidon throws at him, Odysseus keeps on. Even when the shining goddess Calypso keeps him on her island, he yearns for home."

"Indeed, and you, Etta?"

"I admire his cleverness. After all, he was the one who invented the wooden horse. If not for Odysseus, the Trojans might have won the war."

Tante nodded. "So true."

"What a coincidence that our Union Army is now led by Ulysses Grant," I said, "since Ulysses is the Latin form of Odysseus."

Tante frowned. "*Your* army, not mine."

I knew that she and her husband were two of the few Confederate supporters in Comfort. *Tante* even had a female slave, a young girl, who I only glimpsed occasionally. But I also knew that they did not push the issue. So this outburst surprised me.

After an awkward silence, I said, "Well, back to our Odysseus. May I read a verse of his words that capture the man?"

"*Bitte*, Sophie," *Tante* said with a nod.

I read:

"But, if so be that a God on the wine-dark
sea should o'erwhelm me,
That will I bear, for I hold an enduring
heart in my bosom:
For, ere this, have I toiled full much,
and much have I suffered
Both on the sea and in war: but come what
will, I can bear it."

Etta shook her head. "Those words may capture the man but they don't capture me. Who would say, 'For, ere this, have I toiled full much and much have I suffered'? The words are turned inside out."

Tante nodded. "Perhaps I can help, Etta. May I have the book, Sophie?"

I handed it to her, open to Odysseus' words.

"Homer was a poet," she began. "He put words in a different order to keep a rhythm, which can make understanding difficult. Like the line you quoted. You would probably say, 'I have already worked hard and suffered a lot.' But it wouldn't fit the poetic rhythm. It's not musical. Do you see?"

"Ja," Etta said, wrinkling her nose.

I could tell that she saw but did not like.

"Well, like it or not," *Tante* went on, "those are heroic words that we women in Comfort, Texas, must now live by."

That was easy for her to say since her husband was out of danger in Germany. But what if "come what will" means Papa and Eduard do not return? I am not Odysseus. I could not bear it.

I wrote Eduard a letter and included this verse, saying I hoped he, like Odysseus, would endure and return to me. Will the letter ever find him?

Saturday
April 16, 1864

If I thought the appearance of Waldrip's Wolfpack on my birthday was terrifying, what happened today was worse. Never again will I go anywhere without Papa's revolver. But you must wait, dear Reader, for I want to tell it from the beginning.

Every Saturday morning Willie and I walk over to *Tante*'s place to get Pegasus, my pure white horse. Back when our house was burned and we moved to town, *Tante* offered to keep him pastured with her horses.

Then Willie and I ride together across Cypress Creek to our homeplace to pick our kitchen garden for Mama and *Frau* Bremer to use in preparing our meals.

Rosina, our longtime hired girl who lives down the road from our place, helps me take care of the kitchen and flower gardens. Arlis, who Papa hired to help on the farm, is too old to go to war but not too old to take care of the sheep and cattle and manage the butchering when we need beef. He also cleared the place where our house once stood, leaving only the foundation stones. He lives alone in a one-room cabin, not far from Rosina.

But neither Rosina nor Arlis work here on the weekend, so Willie and I are all alone. Until today.

This Saturday was a clear spring day with only a few tall white clouds floating by like great ships on the ocean.

We crossed the creek and started up the long gentle slope, passing by our cornfield that sprouted with green stalks from the recent rains. The rock wall along the road was in good repair, thanks to Arlis. Papa would be happy to see it. Sheep grazed in the meadow below our once house. The lambs were almost as big as their mothers now and had to go down on their knees to suckle. A cool breeze soughed in the liveoaks, and bells on some of the sheep tinkled.

Nothing portended what was to come.

We stopped at the wagon gate, and Willie jumped down to open it. Once inside, I dismounted and left Pegasus to graze in the meadow.

"I'll pick some flowers for Mama," Willie said and off he went to Mama's garden. How that little boy loves flowers.

"There's a jar by the well. Put them in that."

I had forgotten to bring something to hold the vegetables and went out to the barn to get a burlap bag. The doors were open a crack and the padlock hung open with the key in it. I stopped and caught my breath. Usually Arlis bolts and locks the doors and puts the key in a hole in the chinking.

"Arlis? Are you in there?"

No answer.

My heart leaped into pounding. What should I do?

In a moment I said, "Who's there?"

From inside a man said in English, "I mean no harm, Miss." Then he pulled the door open a little.

I caught my breath and stepped back, staring at him. A tall, thin man in a tattered gray uniform of the Confederate Army, he held his cap in hand and bowed. His cheeks were sunken, his eyes pleading.

What did he want? Should I run, grab Willie, and escape on Pegasus? But my legs would not move. I was frozen. All except my heart, which continued its pounding.

And then he spoke again.

"Please, Miss, I'm a deserter and they're looking for me." He shook his head. "I can't fight anymore. I don't want to kill or be killed. I just want to go home to my wife and baby son."

I felt myself relax a bit. He could be Papa or even Eduard. What if one of them tried to escape from the battles and killing? What if he hid in someone's barn and was discovered? By a girl like me? What would I want her to do?

I looked back at Willie. He was happily picking flowers in Mama's garden.

Then I turned to the man.

"Who are you?" I asked in a shaky voice. "And where are you trying to go?"

"Sam Fisher from Zanzenburg, just down the road."

The same one they were looking for at *Tante*'s house.

"That bunch came looking for you in Comfort a few days ago."

"I know, they're on my trail. I'll move on tonight, Miss." He paused. "I just need something to eat – haven't had anything for days."

A feeling of dread came over me as I stood looking at his emaciated face and body. He looked desperate, poor man. If he were Papa or Eduard, what would I want someone to do? I'd want them to bring him food and tell no one.

"Very well, I'll return with some bread and cheese later

today."

"Many thanks."

"Now, would you fetch me a burlap bag out of the wagon?"

He nodded and did so.

"One last request," he said. "If anything happens to me, will you tell my wife, Marie, that I love her and Sammy?"

"Yes." I bit my lips together and took a deep breath. "But I'd rather you tell her."

He gave me a sad smile.

I returned to Willie, who was struggling to draw water at the well. I helped him haul the bucket up and pour water into the jar. Then he added the bouquet of yellow daffodils.

"Do you think Mama will like them?" he asked.

"Ja sure, Willie." All I could think of was the poor man in the barn. What if Waldrip came looking around here?

"What's wrong, Sophie?"

"Nothing, Willie."

He looked at me as if he knew better but I was determined not to tell him, nor would I tell Mama.

"Come, let's gather some vegetables."

While I picked green beans, Willie pulled up carrots. I had taught him how to judge when they were ready, by the size of the carrot's shoulder.

When we were done, I helped Willie into the saddle and handed him the bag and the bouquet. Then I led Pegasus through the gate and mounted him.

Mama had laid out sausage, cheese, and bread for our lunch. Willie set his flowers on the table and we sat on the benches, Mama and Lena on one side, Willie and I on the other.

"*Danke,* Willie," Mama said. "I love that you love flowers. Real men do, you know."

"*Ja,* and I'm a real man, just like Papa."

Mama's blue eyes hardened. "But, hopefully, you will not be as foolish."

My heart plunged. I thought they had fallen in love again after Papa was wounded in the leg. He had even drawn her portrait before leaving. Willie looked down at his plate and said nothing.

"Papa is not foolish," I protested. "He just acts on his beliefs."

"Which are foolish," Mama said.

I stood. "No! They are noble. He loves this country and hates slavery."

"*Ja,* he loves this country more than his wife and family," Mama said bitterly.

I sank down on the bench. "Mama, he had no choice. He either had to fight for the North or the South."

"No fighting," Willie shouted.

I wrapped my arm around him and pulled him close. Lena began to cry and climbed onto Mama's lap.

My mind whirled. All this on top of finding a deserter in our barn. He was another man who acted on his belief. Sick of war and killing, he came home. Was he foolish? Should Papa do that? But then what? Be hunted down by Waldrip's Wolfpack? And hanged?

Mama rocked Lena and stroked her head until she stopped crying.

For a time there was silence.

Finally, Lena wiped her eyes and said, "I like flowers too. Am I a real man?"

We all laughed.

"Nein, Lena, you're a girl," Willie said. "Men pick flowers for girls."

Mama put Lena on the bench beside her, straightened up, and said, "Let us eat, *liebe Kinder,*" dear children. She smoothed a stray lock of blond hair into the braid coiled around her head.

We ate quietly and I without appetite as I thought of Papa and that man in the barn. What is foolish, what is noble?

I cleared the table, set the dishes in a pan of soapy water, and told Mama I would put away the food. She and the little ones lay down for a nap.

Putting sausage, cheese, and bread in a cloth, I tied it up and went outside where Pegasus waited for me. I mounted and we started out. We crossed Cypress Creek and as we came up the hill a terrible sight struck my eyes.

A half dozen horses grazed in our meadow, and a group of men stood around the liveoak that grew beside the place where our house once stood. I used to climb that tree and look down on my world and beyond. Now there were invaders. One of them was tying a rope over a branch.

I gasped. *Gott im Himmel,* it's Waldrip. They're hanging Sam Fisher. I reined in and screamed, "No-o-o-o, don't hang him!"

Waldrip's Wolfpack all turned to look at me, bandannas covering all but their eyes, black hats on their heads.

My mind was reeling frantically. What should I do? Stay where I am? Let it happen? What if he were Papa?

The men stood there. Everything came to a stop. *Can I possibly save the man?* I had to try. I urged Pegasus closer to the gate.

"That is my tree and I don't allow hanging," I shouted.

They all laughed. All except Sam Fisher. He stood on a stool, his arms tied behind his back and a noose around his neck.

"So this is your place?" Waldrip asked.

I nodded.

"And you knew he was here?"

"No," I lied, "but I know who he is." I rode a little closer to the gate. "He lives in Zanzenburg and has a wife and baby."

"Yeah, we know. We was on our way there and saw that your barn door was part open. So we had a look."

Oh no! Why did Sam Fisher leave it open? If only I had closed it, he wouldn't be hanging from my tree. Suddenly it seemed like everything was my fault.

I looked from one man to the other, searching for kindness, and found none. "Have you no pity? How can you be so cruel?"

"That's enough, little lady," Waldrip said. "You go on home before one of my men teaches you a lesson."

Another one of the Wolfpack grinned and said, "I volunteer."

I knew what he meant.

Then Sam Fisher spoke. "Go, Miss, now! And don't forget to tell my wife I love her and Sammy."

Then he turned his eyes upward. "God in Heaven, bless my family and this girl."

My throat tightened and tears streamed down my cheeks. "I won't forget, surely."

"Now!" Waldrip shouted.

I thought my heart would pound out of my chest. I

sucked in a breath and screamed, “No-o-o-o!”

One of his men kicked the stool out from under Sam Fisher. He dropped, his neck twisting, gagging sounds coming from his throat. His body convulsed for a few moments, terrifying moments, and then hung still. Dead.

As I watched, paralyzed by the sight and sounds, Pegasus began to back away. I tightened the reins, turned him toward the creek, and galloped off down the slope.

Later That Night

Even though I am exhausted and heartsick, I must finish writing about today.

When I reached the creek, I reined Pegasus in and dismounted to think what to do. My heart still raced and I panted for breath. I sank down beside the gnarled cypress root that is shaped like an owl's face. Long ago I named him Old Man Owl and even showed him to Eduard. And there, oh happier time, he kissed me.

But now I put my head in my hands and began to weep for Sam, for the awful sight of him dangling from my tree. My body was wracked with sobbing. Could I have done something to save his life? I shook my head. "I don't know, I don't know," I heard myself cry.

Gradually the sobbing loosened its grip on my body and I sat, folded up on myself. All was quiet except for the burbling sound of flowing water. It soothed my heart, and I began to breathe more evenly.

I straightened up and looked at Old Man Owl. He stared at me with one eye, the other closed. In that happier time I thought Old Man Owl was winking because he knew Eduard kissed me. Now as I gazed at his face, Old Man Owl looked weary and about to shut his other eye so as not to see the horror of a man hanged.

I shook my head. This place would never be the same because instead of thinking of Eduard's kiss, I would think of Sam's hanging.

Heaving a sigh, I said, "What now, Old Man Owl? What shall I do?"

If I went home and told Mama, she would just carry on about this horrible wilderness and how she wanted to leave and go back to the safety and elegance of Dresden. I could not face that anger right now. Maybe she was right. This was a horrible place but Papa could never go back to Dresden. He would be punished, maybe hanged, for being involved in the failed revolution against the king. That thought made me feel sick at my stomach.

Old Man Owl stared at me with one eye that suddenly seemed to sharpen and pierce my mind. And then it came to me. Go to *Tante* first and decide what to do in a rational way.

The decision made, I rode on to her house. The children were playing in the front yard, unaware of the awful hanging, much less the finality of it.

As soon as I dismounted and tied Pegasus to the fence post, the children came running to me. They jumped about, begging me to come play hopscotch. To pacify them, I hopped through the squares they had drawn on the packed dirt path. But I did not have the heart for more and stumbled up the steps to the open door.

"That's all for now, *Kinder.*"

Through the screen I saw *Tante* at her desk, writing. She took one look at me and stood. "What has happened, Sophie?"

I entered and told her. She listened with her hand over her heart, gasping now and then.

"Gott im Himmel, liebe Sophie. I'm sorry you had to witness such."

"I feel sorrier for Sam Fisher and his Marie."

Tante nodded and looked thoughtful. "Have you told Elisabet?"

"Nein, not yet. I know what she will say and I don't want to hear it. All I want to do is figure out how to take his body to Zanzenburg for burial."

She nodded. *"Ja,* do you think Arlis would take him down and load the body in your wagon?"

"I think he would."

"If so, then tomorrow morning, early we could go to Zanzenburg and find his wife." *Tante* came and wrapped her arms around me. "You have suffered a trauma, *meine Liebe.* Now you must bear up like Odysseus, and I will be your Athena."

She patted my back and released me. "So, let's you and me ride out to Arlis' cabin before dark and get this started."

"You are like a second mother to me."

"Ach, nein, I have enough children already! I remain your *Tante."*

Finally I could smile.

"Wait for me out front. I'll get Arion."

While I stayed with Pegasus at the gate, she strode out to the barn, followed by Mattie, her slave. *Tante* was the only person in Comfort to own a slave. I hated the idea but loved *Tante,* so we never discussed it.

She whistled for Arion. Soon a black horse trotted up. While *Tante* slipped the bridle over his head, Mattie saddled him.

As we started off, little Herman came running to his mother and raised his arms to her. "I want to go, too."

"Nein, Herman, you must stay with *Oma."*

He started crying.

"Enough now, Herman. Do as I say. I'll be back for supper."

He dropped his arms and stood watching us go, taking jerky little breaths.

We splashed across Cypress Creek and started up the hill. No one was at our homeplace now, only Sam Fisher hanging limp from my tree. One look and I turned toward *Tante.* I saw the horror in her eyes as she took in the scene.

"Mein Gott, what a gruesome sight. Those men are barbarians." She looked away and we continued on through the valley of the Guadalupe River.

The road began to follow alongside the river. As the sun was sinking behind the cypress trees, we arrived at Arlis' cabin, a small log building chinked with stone and mortar, much like our cabin was before Papa added to it.

Arlis must have heard us because he came to the open door. He smoothed his bushy white mustache and beard.

"Well, *guten Abend,* ladies. What brings you here so late? Couldn't be good news."

"Nein, Arlis, it's bad," I said. "Waldrip's Wolfpack just hanged a Confederate deserter from the liveoak beside our old house." I tried to swallow the lump in my throat but could not. Tears started in my eyes, and I wiped them away with the back of my hand. "I was there when they did it, Arlis ... I couldn't make them stop." And then I began to weep.

Tante brought her horse beside me and put her arm around my shoulders. "But you were brave enough to try."

"Gott im Himmel," Arlis said, looking down and shaking his head. "What is this world coming to?"

“To an end, it seems like,” I said.

There was silence for a time. Then Pegasus snorted and stomped his hoof as if to say, *Enough, Sophie.*

I took a deep breath and straightened up. “The man is from Zanzenburg. I promised to go there and tell his wife what happened. And I think he would want me to take his body ...”

Arlis held up his gnarly hand. “You ladies should not be out alone after dark, so I’ll see you to home. Then I’ll cut him down and load his body in the wagon. Tomorrow morning early we can take him to Zanzenburg.”

“You are a gentleman, *Herr* Baumann,” *Tante* said.

“Vielen Dank, Arlis,” I said.

He dipped his head. “Give me a minute to saddle my horse.”

On the way back we agreed to meet at sunrise. As we rode on in silence, darkness fell and a north wind blew in. When we passed by the hanging tree, a gibbous moon was rising over the cypress trees along the creek. In spite of myself I glanced at the lifeless body hanging from a branch I used to climb on. That tree would never be the same. Now, in the dark, all seemed like a nightmare that would not end.

Once home I had to tell Mama what happened. She and the little ones were at supper in *Frau* Bremer’s house, sitting around her big oaken table before a warm fire.

“Sophie!” Willie came running to me and hugged me around the hips.

Mama stared at me. “Where have you been, Sophie? I was worried about you, out alone in the dark.”

The awful news filled my mind but I could not tell it in front of Willie and Lena.

"Oh, I just rode out to our place again to make sure the barn door was locked. Arlis was there, so I wasn't alone."

Mama knew Arlis usually did not work on Saturdays but said no more.

Frau Bremer arose and wrapped her arm around my shoulders, guiding me to the table as if I were lost. Indeed, I did feel lost in my thoughts and rather isolated by the horror I had seen. I looked into her plain but sweet face and felt comforted by her smile.

"Come, Sophie, your supper awaits you." She placed bowls of roast beef, potato salad, and sauerkraut before me. The others resumed eating, and I found that I was hungry as well. Still, an awkward silence fell upon us as if words were held back.

Beside me Willie swung his legs back and forth, and I knew some words wanted to come out. And finally they did.

"Sophie ... what else?"

"What do you mean, what else?"

"I mean, why did it take you so long?"

I sighed. "Oh, Willie, you ask so many questions."

"But ..."

"Willie, eat your dinner," Mama said.

Ignoring her, Willie went on. "But Papa says that's how you learn."

"Willie," Mama said, "there are some things you are too young to learn about."

"Like what, Mama?"

"Like whatever Sophie is not telling us."

Well, that surprised me.

"Is it something about the war? Is Papa dead?"

"Ach, nein, Willie, don't even think that," I said.

"I can't help it."

"But you know he's not fighting, he's drawing battle scenes for the magazine."

"I know." Willie leaned his head against my side, and I patted his leg.

If he knew what I saw ... but I did not want him ever to know such horror. Could I protect him from the sadness in the world?

Later, after Mama and I put the little ones to bed, she and I sat in the armchairs near the fireplace at the other end of the one-room cabin.

When we thought they were asleep, Mama said, "Now, where were you all afternoon?"

So, once again I told about the hanging, reliving the agony of it.

"Mein Gott, Sophie, they could have harmed you."

"I know, Mama, but I had to try to save that man."

"Nein, you did not!" she said, her voice rising. "You should have thought about saving yourself."

"Mama, if you had seen the look on the man's face ..."

"Nein, Sophie, nothing would have kept me there."

"Sophie?" It was Willie.

I arose and went to sit on his bed, like Papa used to do when I had night fears. I caressed his plump cheeks and kissed him on the forehead.

"Go to sleep, sweet Willie," I said. "Everything is all right."

But of course it was not and he knew it. I sat beside him, my hand resting on the blanket covering his chest. I could feel the steady throb of his heart. At last he began to take the long, deep breaths of sleep, and I returned to Mama.

We sat, not talking for a time, just watching the dancing flames of the fire. I could feel the anger Mama held inside herself.

After a time she leaned toward me and whispered, "I cannot stay in this dreadful place. I want to go back to Germany, back to civilization."

She had often expressed this wish to Papa, and he always managed to change her mind. Could I do the same?

"What about Papa? You know he can't go back." It was true.

"But we can."

"And leave Papa?"

"He made his own choice."

"Mama, you know he had no choice. That's what happens in war – no choices. You have to somehow bear the trials, like Odysseus." It felt as if I were the mother and she the child, but I wanted to be Papa's *kleine* Sophie again.

"That is a myth, Sophie, and this is our life."

Sunday
April 17, 1864

By the time *Tante* and I arrived, Arlis had hitched the oxen to our wagon and driven them to the tree where the body lay wrapped in canvas. *Dank dem Himmel.* Thank heaven ... or rather, thank Arlis. I don't think I could bear to see his dead body again.

I picked a red rose from Mama's garden and placed it on top of the canvas, over the place where his heart lay still. Something beautiful to deny the ugly.

Then we helped Arlis carry him to the wagon. At first I hesitated, not wanting to touch the wrappings. But when I looked at *Tante,* she gave me a stern nod that said, *You can bear it, Sophie.* His body was heavier than I imagined, even with us two women at his feet. After we slid him into the wagon, *Tante* and I mounted our horses.

I rode astride, which Pegasus and I prefer. My new blue floral was long enough so that my legs were not exposed. I had a straw bonnet with blue ribbons tied under my chin. Appropriately, *Tante wore* a black silk with matching bonnet and rode sidesaddle.

The first rays of sunlight shone over the treetops along Cypress Creek as we left our homeplace and turned west on the road to Zanzenburg. *Tante* and I led the way while Arlis followed, walking beside the oxen with a prod stick to keep them moving. Even so, oxen go at a slow pace and even slower when pulling a heavy wagon. It would probably be noon before we arrived, but I was in no hurry to break the sad news to Sam's wife. I dreaded the moment when we reached her. The only consolation I had were his words of love.

After we had gone a ways, Arlis said, "What was this man's name?"

"Sam ... Sam Fisher," I said. "Did you know him?"

"Nein, but I know someone who would. The post office is in his home on this side of the river. His wife runs it now that he's serving in the Confederate Army."

"Ja, I know the family too," *Tante* said. "They have wealth and connections. Jennie Ganahl surely knows everyone in Zanzenburg. She can direct us."

It sounded like finding his wife would be easy, but telling her, seeing her look at his body .... If only I could have persuaded Waldrip to let him go. Did I try hard enough? Or was I more intent on saving myself? Doubts began to creep into my mind. *Maybe I could have saved his life.*

The road curved closer to the Guadalupe River where giant cypress roots coiled like snakes over the bank. We were silent for a long time, the only sounds being the rush of water, creaking of the wagon, and an occasional blow from the horses' nostrils, as if saying, *Are we almost there?*

Finally, I could hold back my doubts no longer.

"Tante, do you think I could have saved him?" I asked quietly so Arlis would not hear.

She drew a sharp breath. *"Ach, liebe* Sophie, *nein!* Not possible. Those men have no pity, no qualms. They get power from killing. Even though they may not hang women, I think they would have no qualms about ravishing a pretty one who tried to interfere with their intent. You told me one of them threatened you." She shook her head. "*Nein,* you did all you could."

"*Ja,* but it wouldn't have killed me." Still, I shuddered at the thought.

"It could have. In any case, you would be as good as dead. And they would have hanged him anyway. So you would both be dead."

I nodded. She made sense, but I would never know for sure.We rode on and I turned to Arlis, wondering if he was tired. After all, he was an old man in his sixties. "Are you all right, Arlis?"

"*Ja,* sure, *Fräulein.* Walking keeps me young." He paused for a moment. "What do you hear from your papa?"

"Nothing lately. The last letter we got said he was going to Chattanooga to draw battle scenes. That was last fall."

"*Ja,* the Union won that one," he said. "General Grant is hard to beat."

I nodded, although with thousands of men killed and wounded or taken prisoner, neither side won. From what I read in the *Zeitung,* many of the wounded died or had an arm or leg amputated. And being a prisoner was almost sure death from starvation or disease.

Tante remained silent. Her husband was safe in Germany. What could she say? Especially since the two of them favored the Confederacy.

Around noon we came to the mouth of Turtle Creek, and there stood the Ganahl house, a wide one-story building with a gallery across the front and double doors in the center. Beyond the house, horses grazed in a meadow.

Beautiful, sleek horses.

"They raise thoroughbreds," *Tante* said. "Unfortunately the redskins like to steal them."

Redskins, that's what she calls Indians. I don't like that word. My Indian friend, the Comanche chief, did not have red skin. Not only that, he helped me save Papa when he was wounded on the Nueces River.

The problem is that there are different bands of Indians, some friendly, some not. Now that the frontier forts have been abandoned, the unfriendly Indians are back. So we have war in both directions, Indians to the west and Confederates to the east. People are weary of it, those of us left behind and those fighting in the war. More and more deserters are going home to their families — only to be hanged, like Sam Fisher.

We dismounted at the fence, a distance from the house, while a collie on the gallery barked at us. Soon a slave woman came out and quieted him.

"Wait there," she called. "I'll get my mistress."

When a lady, followed by a young girl, stepped out the door, *Tante* said, "Jennie, it is Emma Altgelt and friends."

"Oh my goodness, Emma. What brings you here?"

"Sad news, I'm afraid."

Mistress Ganahl hurried to us, her long skirts swishing. She stopped and stared at the wrapped body, her hand covering her heart.

"Who?"

"Sam Fisher," I said. "Do you know his family?"

She gasped and for a moment could not speak. Then ..."Oh, dear God, I thought maybe it was my Charles."

"Jennie, *Tante* said, "this is my young friend, Sophie Guenther. She was a witness to the hanging and protested ... to no avail."

I nodded and told her the story and how he asked me to give his love to his wife and little boy.

"Yes, Sophie, I do know his wife Marie and baby boy. They live in Zanzenburg proper, across the river." She turned back toward the house and called the slave woman to come.

"Ora, show them the way to the Fisher home."

"Yes, Mistress."

"May I go too, Mama?" the little girl asked.

"No, Charlisa, you're too young."

Tante thanked Mistress Ganahl, and we crossed the low-water bridge to Zanzenburg, a town smaller than Comfort with scattered houses and a general store. Children played in the front yards while women and a few old men sat on their galleries and watched us go by.

"Where are you headed?" one man in a rocking chair asked.

"To the Fisher place," *Tante* answered.

"Oh no, it's Sam," a woman said and covered her mouth.

The creaking of our wagon brought more people out to see what was happening, and some began to follow us.

We came to a house where a young woman stood on the gallery like a statue, holding a baby in her arms.

"Here we are," Ora said.

Marie, no doubt, I thought.

All at once she came alive, ran toward us, threw open the gate, and stopped beside the wagon, staring at the wrapped body.

She shook her head. "You're not bringing my Sam, are

you?"

With a wrenching in my belly, I nodded. "If you are Marie ... yes."

Her mouth fell open and she looked at me, her eyes unbelieving. She threw back her head and screamed. "No-o-o-o-o!." The baby started crying, and one of the town's women came and took him in her arms. Marie scrambled into the wagon, screaming and weeping. "No, it can't be you, Sam, it can't." She opened the wrapping at the top and gasped.

"Oh, Sam, no-o-o-o-o." She lay down beside him, wrapped her arms around his body, and wept.

I put my face in my hands and wept too. This is how it is to lose a loved one. No one can do anything. No one can bring him back. He is gone forever.

People around us did not move, did not speak. Women dabbed at their eyes with handkerchiefs.

I dismounted and stood beside the wagon. "Marie?"

She lifted her head, staring at me with watery eyes.

"Marie ... I'm Sophie Guenther." I swallowed hard to get rid of the lump in my throat. "Yesterday morning I rode out to our homeplace near Comfort and found your husband hiding in our barn. We don't live there anymore because our house burned down."

She climbed out of the wagon and grasped me by the shoulders, her eyes frantic. "What? Tell me what happened?"

"He said he deserted from the Confederate Army. I warned him that Waldrip's Wolfpack was looking for him in town, that he should move on for his own safety. He was hungry, and I promised to bring him something to eat."

Marie began to slowly shake her head as if to deny

what I was about to say.

"When I returned a band of vigilantes was ... preparing to hang him. I pleaded with them to stop but they threatened me. His last request was that I tell you he loved you and the baby."

Her face twisted with pain and tears streamed down her cheeks. "He shouldn't have deserted but I know why he did."

"Why?" I asked.

"He wanted to see his son. In his last letter Sam said he was afraid he would be killed without ever laying eyes on him."

Marie again shook her head in disbelief. "I had a husband and now I don't."

I felt a pang in my chest as the awful finality of her words echoed in the air. *I had a husband and now I don't, now I don't.* Nothing could ever bring him back. What if this were Papa or Eduard?

The woman holding the baby brought him to Marie. "But you have little Sammy."

Marie took him in her arms and held him close, kissing the top of his head.

Arlis stepped up. "My condolences, Madam. May we carry your husband into the house?"

I noticed he did not say your husband's *body,* which was kind.

She looked up and nodded.

Other women gathered around and, together with *Tante* and Arlis, we carried Sam into the house and laid him on a table, still wrapped. His life was over. Finished. The finality of death overwhelmed me. No one I loved had died. How could I bear it?

Marie sat in a rocking chair on the gallery and rocked

Sammy. He knew nothing of death, only the love of his mother. Women took chairs out of the house and sat with her. Others brought pitchers of watered wine, bread, and cheese from their homes. They told stories about Sam, how he loved to race his horse with other boys in town and often won. How, after his parents died, he took over his father's business as the town's blacksmith. More and more stories, which seemed to comfort Marie and even make her smile.

Then *Tante* leaned close to me. "I think it's time for us to go."

I agreed. As I stood watching Marie rock Sammy, I could not think what to say. There were no adequate words.

Tante said, "May you find peace, Marie."

I did not think peace was what she wanted. What, then? Sam — Sam alive, wrapping his arms around her and the baby. She wanted him back to love and love her. But she couldn't have him back. All she had was Sammy.

"May Sammy bring you joy," I said.

She gave me a trembly smile.

We rode home in silence most of the way, thinking our own thoughts. Even though *Tante* said *no,* I wondered if I could have saved him by being bolder.

The sun was setting behind the cypress trees when we arrived at our homeplace and said goodbye to Arlis.

After leaving Pegasus in *Tante*'s barn for the night, I stopped by Etta's house and told her all that had happened.

She stared at me openmouthed. Then she hugged me tight.

"*Ach,* Sophie, I can't even imagine how Marie feels."

"I can ... a little bit. It's like your insides have been emptied out. Like you are hollow."

"Well, I don't want it to happen to us."

"But you and I know it will."

Etta shook her head. "Not for a long, long time."

"I hope."

As I walked on home I thought, *hope is not enough.* It's weak. It does not make anything happen or not happen. Still it's necessary. Otherwise I would just sink into a black hole of despair.

And then it came to me. Hope is something that supports whatever is in my power to do. I can't save Papa or Eduard, and I can't make the war end. So what can I do? I can try to keep our family safe until what I hope for happens.

Sunday
May 1, 1864

We did not celebrate May Day with dancing around a Maypole like we used to when there were men to cut down a tree and dig a hole for it. And *Herr* Schimmelpfennig was not here to play his violin while we danced and wove our ribbons around the pole.

So Willie had an idea. He and I picked wildflowers and walked around town delivering little bouquets to our friends.

Frau Bremer gave us a hug and said, "*Liebe Kinder,* you bring joy to my life."

I could not help thinking back to that May Day two years ago when Eduard said to me, "You should have been the May Queen."

He meant instead of Christine, the most beautiful girl in our village. And she knew it. She already had breasts but I did not. I guess queens need breasts!

But now I could be queen for I have become a woman. What would Eduard think of me? I will write a letter to him this very night and remind him of that day. Should I also tell him about the hanging and how I wonder if I could have saved Sam?

Friday
June 3, 1864

School is over for the summer. We finished reading *The Odyssey,* and all I can say is that I am happy Odysseus finally found his way home to Penelope. After twenty years she did not recognize him in his beggar's clothing, nor did the suitors, who were drinking and feasting in his hall.

Penelope had finally decided that Odysseus would never return, so she ordered a contest for that evening. She swore to marry whichever man among them could string her husband's great horn bow and shoot an arrow through the rings of twelve axes standing in a line. It thrilled me when the beggar proved himself by being the only man among them strong enough and skilled enough to do so. It was then that Penelope realized that the beggar was her Odysseus.

But did he really have to kill all her suitors, one hundred of them? If Mama had suitors, Papa would send them off but not *kill* them. I guess those were more violent times — or were they? In our war men have killed each other by the thousands. Sometimes I wonder if we will ever learn to live in peace.

I should not say *we* when I mean *men.* We women in Comfort curse the war as we wait for word from our men and wonder who will return and who will not.

Wednesday
June 29, 1864

I promised myself only to write about significant thoughts and happenings in this journal. And today one of those happened.

On Wednesdays mail and supplies arrive at Faltin Mercantile, brought from San Antonio. Sometimes very little, sometimes more, depending on the blockade runners.

Mama sent me there with her reticule to buy coffee beans and see if we might have a letter from Papa. We have had no word from him since my birthday. It seemed like every woman in town was there or sent someone, like Etta and me.

She greeted me at the door. "Sophie, want to go swimming this afternoon?"

That sounded very nice since the day was already growing hot. There is a swimming hole on Cypress Creek where 8th Street ends at the water's edge. Young children swim in their underclothes but girls our age just wade in the creek.

"Sure, I'll bring Willie, too."

"Gut! Tell him to get ready for splashing." Then she held up a letter. "This came from Papa, so I have to run home. Mama will be so-o-o happy."

"I'm glad for you, Etta. I hope we have a letter too."

"I think I saw something in your mailbox. Maybe it's

from your husband! You know, E.M."

Some of the women who were sitting on the front gallery chuckled. How Etta loved to tease me about Eduard. It used to irritate me but no more. Now, I want everyone to know that he is my true love.

"I sure wish there were some boys around here to kiss," she went on.

I laughed, remembering how she kicked mean old Thomas when he bullied me at school one day. "I thought you preferred to *kick* boys."

"Ha! It all depends on the boy, Sophie, as you know."

She turned, leaped off the gallery, arms flying, and ran down the path and out the gate. "See you this afternoon."

I remembered when Eduard kissed me goodbye and went off to war. No boy had ever kissed me. I was only thirteen and he fifteen, but it sealed my heart forever.

So now I hurried inside the store, eager to see if the letter was from Papa or Eduard. It was crowded with women buying coffee, gossiping, and reading their mail. *Frau* Faltin, a slim woman with dark hair parted in the middle and pulled back into a bun, motioned me to come to the post office window at the end of the room.

She smiled as she handed me the letter. "From your papa, I believe. Your mother will surely be happy."

Though I felt relieved to know Papa was alive, something sank inside me. There was nothing from Eduard.

"Danke, Frau Faltin." I hesitated for a moment.

"Just one letter?"

She smiled. "Be thankful, Sophie. Some women got none."

"I hope you got one from your husband."

"Not this time, but I know he is safe in Germany."

How I wished that Papa and Eduard were somewhere safe too. Slipping the letter into Mama's reticule, I said goodbye and started for the door, thinking only how I yearned to hear from Eduard.

"Wait, Sophie," she said. "Did you not want coffee beans? We received a nice supply but it will soon be gone."

"Ach, ja, the coffee."

Even though the letter begged to be opened, I waited in line at the counter where the Faltins' daughter was weighing the beans. Talk went on all around me but I was inside my mind. All I could think about was the letter. Where was Papa? Maybe he had some news about Eduard. I longed to open the envelope and read the letter but it was addressed to Mama.

After buying coffee, I ran home. Mama sat on the front gallery with Lena in her lap while Willie drew a picture of a horse in the dirt with a stick. He was always drawing in the dirt because there was a shortage of paper.

"Just like Papa," I told him as I passed, waving the letter for Mama to see.

He grinned and followed me to the gallery.

Mama gasped. "Oh, Sophie, let it be good news."

"Well, it means he is alive!"

My heart raced from running and anticipation. I handed her the letter and sat on the edge of the gallery with Willie.

Mama's hands shook as she carefully opened the envelope.

"Read it, read it," Willie said.

"Patience, Willie," Mama said. "I don't want to tear the envelope." Then she unfolded the letter and read.

New York
May 28, 1864

Meine Lieben!

I hope that you are well. Thank you for your joint letter of February 14. I was glad to hear that Sophie is helping Emma teach Willie and other children to read. And I enjoyed Willie's drawing of Max. All in all, the letter lifted my spirits.

Still, I worry about your living in a village without men. Sophie, you must keep the pistol handy and loaded as I taught you and be the strong one.

You will all be relieved to know that I am alive, which is more than I can say for many poor soldiers on both sides. War is unspeakably horrid, and I must draw it, battle after battle, day after day.

Harper's Weekly recently sent me to Spotsylvania in Virginia. The battles there went on for two weeks and I am told that 32,000 men died! It is insanity.

I do not know of Eduard's whereabouts but hope for his safety — though there is no such thing in war.

The only good news I have to write is that Lincoln was nominated for a second term. But if the Union does not win this war soon, I doubt he will be elected.

I think of you, Elisabet, Sophie, Willie, and *kleine* Lena every hour. If only I could embrace and kiss you. As soon as this war is over, I will return.

Yours,
Friedrich (Papa)

Mama shook her head. "Why doesn't he just come home now?"

I scarcely knew what to say or think about Papa's letter. It was a relief to know that he was alive but awful to hear about so many deaths.

"You know he can't come home, Mama. Think what just happened to the deserter. At least Papa is determined to return as soon as the war is over."

She frowned and said, "That doesn't mean he *will*, Sophie!"

Willie crawled over to her, sat on his knees, and put his head on her lap. *"Bitte,* Mama, no fighting."

She ruffled his blond curls and smiled. *"Ja, mein Liebling."*

Mama was right. Papa might not come home. Sometimes I think if this war does not end soon, she will make good on her threat to return to Germany, even though Papa cannot. And then what would I do? Would I stay here or go with her?

Nothing more was said about Papa's letter, but I could not get it out of my mind. *Keep the pistol handy and loaded and be the strong one,* he said. He knew that Mama did not want to do either.

I remember when Papa left to go to war he said, *"Fortis fortuna adiuvat."* Fortune favors the brave. Odysseus knew that, but what about Hector in *The Iliad?* He was brave and he was slain. What am I to believe? The truth is, I have no choice. I must be brave — like *Tante* when those ruffians came to her door. I must think like a soldier's daughter.

That afternoon as Etta, Willie, and I walked down 8th Street toward the creek, I heard other children laughing and shouting and longed to be so carefree. But I have always been a worrier. I worried about Papa when he was here because of his editorial cartoons for the San Antonio *Zeitung* that sided with the North — even as Texas seceded from the Union. Now I worry about him and Eduard, somewhere in the midst of battles. Will there ever come a time of no worries?

"What did your papa have to say about the war?" I asked Etta. As our village pharmacist, he had joined the medical corps in the Confederate Army — not because he was in favor of slavery but because it was the easier way. And probably a wiser way than Papa and Eduard took.

"I don't want to hear any more about the war!" Willie exclaimed.

"Then run ahead and wait for us on the bank," I told him.

As he scampered away, Etta continued.

"He said the field hospitals are crowded and unbelievably filthy. If men don't die from wounds, they die from disease." She paused. "What about yours?"

"He said 32,000 men died fighting in only two weeks! He calls it insanity."

Etta shook her head. "I wonder if any men will be left after the war."

"Ach, let's stop talking about it, like Willie says. Sometimes I think he's wiser than me."

"Ja, let's go swim!" Etta shouted.

Together we ran to the banks of the creek. There, Willie sat on the root of an ancient cypress tree in his drawers, ready to wade in.

"Come on, Sophie!"

For the moment I abandoned my worries about the war, along with my shoes and stockings. Etta and I each took Willie by the hand and waded into the shallows. He squealed as he lowered himself up to his neck in the cool, clear water, which ran over my feet and drenched the hem of my dress.

"Look here, Willie," Etta said, letting go of his hand and splashing water on his face.

Then Willie and I splashed water on her. She laughed and splashed me until my dress was damp and cool on my skin. Finally we crawled out and sat on the roots, where Etta and I wrung out the hems of our skirts.

For that moment, thoughts of the war and Indians were washcd away.

Friday
September 16, 1864

The rest of the summer passed peacefully, and school commenced early this month. *Tante* has Etta and me reading about the Italian Renaissance and Leonardo da Vinci and Michelangelo. The book has a drawing of Leonardo on the title page with his piercing eyes and long, gray beard. It is a relief to read about another time and place and forget about the war.

But last night we had a frightening reminder.

Now that our village has no men to protect us, hostile Indians grow bold. They have stolen horses and cattle and even some women and children from isolated farms north and west of here. Last night they came to Comfort.

I awoke to a high, screaming whinny, coming from the direction of *Tante*'s house. Could it be Pegasus? I put on my slippers and stepped out on the gallery. The full moon had risen.

NNNNN-hhhhh, NNNNN-hhhhh.

Ja, it was either Pegasus or *Tante*'s horse.

I leaped off the gallery and ran down the street. At the end of Main I stopped at the rock wall in terror. There, some twenty paces away, an Indian was putting a harness on Pegasus. Another sat astride a paint horse.

"Pegasus!" I yelled.

He tried to back away and reared. But the Indian

pulled him down, and both turned to me.

Then I saw *Tante*'s slim figure in the moonlight. Wrapped in a robe, she stood outside her front door, pointing her pistol at them with both hands, waiting for a clear shot.

What to do? My heart hammered as I stood in my white nightdress, practically naked with nothing to defend myself, in spite of what Papa wrote.

Then I remembered what Papa told me a long time ago. I shouted the Spanish word for German at the top of my lungs. *"ALEMÁN ... ALEMÁN!"*

If they were Comanches, they would know about the treaty with Germans and leave us alone.

For a moment no one moved or made a sound. The full moon shone down on us as if we were statues. Pegasus looked like the white mustang that the Indians call Spirit Horse. No wonder they wanted him.

But they were not Comanches and Pegasus was not all they wanted.

Using him as a shield from *Tante*'s aim, the two started toward me!

Gott im Himmel! My heart leaped into pounding.

Tante raised her pistol to the sky and fired.

But they kept coming, coming to carry me away! To ravish me. My legs trembled and threatened to buckle. One word shouted in my head. *RUN!* I turned and ran, stumbling and then falling. Any minute I would feel rough hands clutching me. I scrambled up, gasping for breath, and looked back.

NNNNN-hhhhh. Pegasus reared and knocked his captor to the ground with his hooves. He lay stunned. Quickly the other Indian leaped from his horse, grabbed Pegasus' reins, and pulled him down. Then, flinging the wounded man over his horse, he mounted, swung his horse about, and galloped off toward Cypress Creek, pulling Pegasus along beside them as a shield.

Tante fired again.

"Pegasus!" I called, "Pegasus!"

He tried to turn back but the Indian jerked on his reins.

Pegasus had saved me but could not save himself.

Tears streamed down my cheeks and I put my face in my hands and wept. It seemed that everyone and everything I loved, Papa, Eduard, our home, my horse, were being taken from me. Even my maidenhood had been threatened, perhaps my life. Oh, what was to become of us?

Tante ran to the rock wall, and I hurried to her. *"Ach, Liebchen,"* she said breathlessly. "I was afraid they were going to take you, too! What are you doing out here, almost naked and without a pistol? They could have carried you off if Pegasus hadn't kept them from it."

"I know. It was stupid of me. I'll never go anywhere again without Papa's pistol."

"Gut," she said.

I hesitated. *When Mama hears about this, she will be determined to go back to Germany as soon as possible, in spite of Papa.*

"Let's not tell Mama about the Indians threatening me," I said. "I'm afraid she will make us leave Comfort."

Tante studied me for a moment, she in her modest wrapper and I in my thin white nightdress. I shivered, more from fright than the cool air.

"Your mother is a dear friend, and I cannot keep such

a secret from her."

"Even if I promise never to do anything so foolish again?"

"Nein, Sophie. All the women in our village need to know what happened tonight. If those redskins are stealing our horses, they'll steal women and children too, as you saw. We need to be prepared. Every woman in Comfort needs to carry a gun at all times and know how to shoot it."

She paused, thinking, and then went on. "So, I'll put up a notice in Faltin's in the morning for all to meet Saturday at the schoolhouse at ten o'clock. Can you and Etta spread the news around the village as well?"

I nodded while my mind tried to grasp the fact that Pegasus was gone. He was a gift from Papa for my tenth birthday, an Arabian bought in San Antonio. I would never have a horse like him again. He had carried me some ninety miles out to the Nueces River to find Papa when he was wounded while trying to escape to Mexico and join the Union Army.

"Do you think I'll ever see Pegasus again?" I asked.

"Only a miracle could make that happen, Sophie." She paused. "I'm just grateful that they failed to take you too."

I reached across the rock wall and hugged her. "Because of you and Pegasus."

Then she held me by the shoulders. "Now, run home, bar the door, and get in bed. Tomorrow you must tell Elisabet what happened."

Back home, I could not sleep for the longest time. My hands and knees hurt from falling in the street. And my mind whirled. Would Mama be angry with me? What would she say and do? Would Willie and Lena be scared?

When at last I slept, it seemed like Mama was up fixing our breakfast as soon as my eyes closed. I sat up in bed and saw that the little ones were still asleep, so I put on my wrapper and joined Mama in front of the fireplace. She was hanging the coffee pot on a hook over the fire.

"Mama," I whispered, "I have to tell you what happened last night."

She straightened up and looked at me with a frown. "What, Sophie?"

"Some Indians stole Pegasus."

She stared at me for a moment, her blue eyes sharp, her blond hair hanging below her shoulders and glowing in the firelight. "How do you know?"

"Because I heard him whinny and went to *Tante*'s pasture."

"You went out in the dark?" she asked, her frown deepening.

"Ja, I know it was foolish."

She nodded. "You're just like your father."

"I haven't told you the worst, Mama. Promise you won't be angry."

Her mouth fell open, as if she could not believe there was more. "I cannot promise, Sophie."

Just then Willie wandered in from behind the folding screen that separates our sleeping quarters, wearing his white nightshirt. "What's the worst, Sophie?"

I knelt down to look him in the eye. It would be easier to tell him instead of Mama, and maybe she would not react so strongly.

"Well, *Liebchen,* first some Indians stole Pegasus last

night."

Willie looked at me with sad eyes and then wrapped his arms around my neck. *"Nein,* Sophie!"

"Ja, I am afraid it's true, and that is not the worst."

He stepped back and waited for the worst.

"The Indians tried to capture me but Pegasus knocked one of them down and they fled."

"Hurray for Pegasus!" Willie shouted, jumping about and clapping his hands.

Lena toddled in, sleepy eyed. "I hungry."

Mama picked her up. *"Ja, meine Liebchen."* She carried Lena to the pantry cabinet, gave her a chunk of cornbread, and returned to us.

"Sophie, I cannot believe you exposed yourself to such danger. If you are going to be as foolish as your father, then we have to leave this place."

"Mama, I know it was foolish and I promise never to go anywhere without Papa's pistol."

"Nein, I am not going to live in the wilderness where people have to carry weapons and my children are in danger of being kidnapped by barbarians. I'm just not!"

"Where then?" I asked.

"Germany, of course."

"Mama, you know that is not possible."

"Anything is possible if you want it enough."

"Not with the blockade of the ports," I reminded her.

Willie looked from one of us to the other. When there was a pause he said, "I don't want to go to Germany. I want to stay here and wait for Papa to come home."

Mama ruffled his blond curls. *"Liebchen,* your Papa would not want us to stay here if it's dangerous. Besides, we can return when the war is over."

But I knew that once back in Germany, she would never return. And I knew that Papa could not join us.

Willie looked up at me with a question in his eyes that I could not answer.

On the way to school Etta joined us. When she saw the look on my face, she stepped in front of me, hands on hips, and made us stop. "What's happened?"

It was Willie who told her. "Indians stole Pegasus and tried to kidnap Sophie but Pegasus knocked one of them down and they ran off."

Her mouth fell open. *"Nein,* Willie, you're just trying to scare me."

He shook his curly head and looked at me.

"Sadly it's true," I said and told her the story. By that time we had reached *Tante*'s house.

She was on the porch welcoming children as if nothing had happened. As we greeted her she said, "Not a word."

I leaned over Willie and whispered, "Promise?"

He looked up at me. "I promise, Sophie."

I could not concentrate on teaching the little ones, and the Renaissance held no interest for me. Pegasus was gone and nothing else mattered. Willie was restless, too, as if he yearned to tell the story and had to hold it in.

After school Etta, Willie, and I walked from house to house, telling women about the meeting. It helped that a few bolstered my hope that he might find his way back. "Horses know the way home, even if our men don't," one said.

Saturday September 17, 1864

I think every woman came. It was a sunny, clear day that felt like autumn even though the solstice does not arrive until next week. Mama and another lady volunteered to watch the children at play outside while the rest of us met in the log schoolhouse. She never cared for meetings and frightening talk about guns. Willie begged to come with me but I told him *nein*. He poked out his lower lip and stomped his foot.

Women greeted one another and stepped inside. I looked around for Etta but did not see her, so I entered. *Tante* sat at the teacher's desk at one end of the room, watching as women took their seats on the benches. Even though a small, girlish woman, *Tante* had an aura of authority about her, maybe because of the way her chin tilted upward. She wore a blue silk dress with a gold brooch at her neck. Her dark hair was neatly coiled atop her head.

She gestured for me to sit on the front row, and I saved a place for Etta who soon came and plopped down beside me, breathless.

"Mama made me finish drying the dishes, so I had to run all the way ... thought I was late."

Tante stood then, very erect, and rang her school bell to call the meeting to order.

"You're just in time!" I whispered.

When all was quiet, *Tante* began.

"Brave women of Comfort, we gather this morning to determine how we can protect ourselves from the emboldened redskins." She glanced at me. "As you know, Sophie's beloved Pegasus was stolen from my pasture Thursday night under a full moon. Even worse, Sophie herself was threatened by them." She paused, looking about the room. "And in my opinion, we are all in danger of being stolen. So, let us discuss our firearms, our ability to use them, and a warning signal. I open the floor to you." She sat down and waited.

At first, no one spoke up.

"Come now, ladies, we must be the men of this village," *Tante* added.

There was a ripple of laughter and I turned around to look at the audience. Then Etta's mother stood and broke the silence. She had the same frizzy red hair as her daughter but *Frau* Lange's braids were coiled around her head.

"*Ja,* I agree. We must defend ourselves. My husband left his six-shooter here for me for that reason, though I've never fired the weapon."

"I'm glad you brought that up, Ida," *Tante* said, "because I would be happy to instruct anyone in loading and shooting their firearms. After all, I am a soldier's daughter." She gestured to me. "And I imagine Sophie would too. She is an excellent shot."

I stood. "*Ja,* when my papa was threatened by ruffians, I asked him to teach me to use his pistol. And after the hanging I witnessed back in April, I promised myself I would carry it everywhere. Then Thursday night

I forgot — not that I could have saved my horse — but I might have been able to save myself had Pegasus not kept the Indians from kidnapping me. So, keep your firearm loaded and with you."

"Indeed, Sophie," *Tante* said. "Now why don't we discuss the firearms we each have and decide on lessons for any woman who needs them."

One after another, the women stood and told what firearms they had. A few said they wanted lessons, and *Tante* wrote down their names, dipping her quill into an ink jar.

"And finally, can we agree on a warning signal?" *Tante* asked. "I suggest the same one our men agreed on earlier, one long blast on a cow's horn."

There were murmurs of agreement.

"So may I hear *ja* or *nein?*"

It was unanimous. I would need to ask Arlis for one because ours was destroyed in the fire like everything else.

"Before we go I have a few words to say."

I turned to see who had spoken. It was *Frau* Weber, a handsome blond woman with a cleft chin and tight mouth. She stood in the middle of the room, frowning.

"We wouldn't be at war if the people in Texas, even some of us Germans, had not voted to secede from the Union!"

There was an audible gasp. I glanced at *Tante.* Her lips were clamped and her eyes hooded.

Frau Weber continued. "Our husbands would not be fighting and dying on the battlefields while yours, Emma, is safe in Germany."

Tante drew in a deep breath and stood. "*Meine liebe*

Bertha, first of all, my husband and founder of our village ..." She paused to let those words sink in. "... returned to Germany to care for his ailing father, not to escape the war."

There were mutterings among the women. Did they doubt her words? I did.

One time she told Mama that Ernst left because he had a weak constitution and could not survive the harsh life of a soldier. So what was the truth? I think *Tante* encouraged him to flee for his life, and I cannot blame her for that. I only wish Papa had done the same thing, like *Herr* Faltin as well.

"Second," *Tante* went on, "my husband did not vote to secede, nor would I, even if I had the right. Indeed, our county was one of only a few that voted against secession. Nevertheless, my sympathies are with the South. I believe, as did he, that each state should decide whether having slaves is legal. Great plantations cannot be run without them."

Why not? I wanted to say. *Why not pay workers rather than own them?* But I could not argue with *Tante,* not here in front of all the women of our village. It would be like a betrayal of the friendship between our families. Long ago *Tante* and her husband gave us a place to stay when our house was burned down after Papa left to join the Union Army. No, I could never criticize her for owning a slave.

"Still," she went on, "I appreciate your concern but feel that now, in our village without men, we need to plan our defense together even though our opinions may pull us apart. After all, we are civilized, educated women who know how to discuss our differences without fighting.

Sometimes I wonder if men have figured that out!"

A few women chuckled. Others talked between themselves.

Frau Weber said, "Perhaps not, Emma. But I am relieved to hear that your husband did not vote for secession."

Tante knew that most women in the village were Unionists, even though some of their husbands took the so-called easy way out and joined the Confederate Army rather than be persecuted by the vigilantes that roamed the land. Actually there was no easy way out. Men had to join one side or the other or hide for the duration of the war.

Tante nodded. "May all our husbands return to us and peace be upon the land."

"So be it," said *Frau* Weber and the meeting ended.

Etta leaped up. "Whew, I'm glad that's over."

Tante smiled at Etta and me. "All's well that ends well."

But all has not ended well, I thought. Pegasus is gone. Papa and Eduard are gone, and we are threatened ...

Tuesday
October 11, 1864

We were in school this afternoon when the miracle happened.

My little students were napping while the four older ones worked on their sums at the dining table with *Tante*. Etta and I sat together on the couch, reading Goethe's *Faust*.

We hate the man Faust. He is no Odysseus! He seduces Gretchen and ruins her life forever. Maybe *Tante* assigned us to read this book as a cautionary tale for our own lives. But I would never let a man be intimate with me — only the one I marry. *Ja,* I'm thinking of Eduard, dear Reader. And I don't believe Etta would either. She would probably punch him and kick his shins.

"I *hate* this book," Etta whispered.

"Me too," I replied but we continued reading out of duty to *Tante*.

The front door stood open to the warm, sunny day. All was quiet. I felt my eyelids drooping until …

A long blast on a cow's horn sounded, then another and another.

Children raised their heads, *Tante* stood, I caught my breath as Etta and I leaped up and ran to the door. Unsnapping the holster on my belt, I pulled out Papa's small pistol. *Tante* edged past us, her gun in hand, and stepped out the door. I followed her.

Instead of danger, what we saw was my Comanche friend, Chief Tsena and his wife Anawakeo with their young son on the horse behind her, reined up outside the gate. The chief held a rope tied to ... Pegasus!

"*Jefe* Tsena!" I called to him. Chief Tsena.

Frau Weber stood on her front gallery across the street, holding her pistol in both hands, pointed at Tsena.

"*Nein,* he's my friend!" I shouted. "Don't shoot! He's the one who helped me save Papa."

She lowered her gun, and I put mine back in the holster, as did *Tante.*

"Your miracle has come to pass, *meine Liebe,*" she said.

I nodded but kept my eyes on Pegasus. "Would you keep the children back while I go out to our visitors? I don't want them to alarm Pegasus."

"Of course." *Tante* moved to hold the screen door shut.

"Sophie, can I go with you?" It was Willie.

"Ja, Liebchen."

Tante opened the screen and I took his hand. Together we walked along the swept path of the flower garden and out the gate. Slowly and silently. Women in nearby houses up the street stood on their galleries, their guns still in hand.

Pegasus sniffed the air and whinnied.

It sent a thrill through my body. Willie and I came close and I stroked Peg's snow-white forehead. When Willie raised his little hand, Pegasus lowered his head so he could reach.

I put my arms around his neck. "Oh, Peg, I was afraid I'd never see you again."

He flicked his ears as if to say, *It's good to be back.*

Then I turned to Chief Tsena who was watching me with a smile on his lean face. Sitting erect on his red horse, he looked noble in his fringed leggings and silver breastplate.

Anawakeo smiled too. Her long black hair was parted in the middle and held in place with a beaded headband. Nistiuma, their son, sat behind her on the paint horse. He was about the same age as Willie, and wore a buckskin breechcloth.

German and English words whirled in my mind, words they could not understand. I knew that Tsena spoke a little Spanish. So I put my hand over my heart and said some words Papa had taught me. *"Gracias, mis amigos."* Thanks, my friends.

Tsena nodded and Anawakeo smiled.

I wanted to ask how he found Pegasus but had not the words.

By this time women had gathered from all around and stared at Chief Tsena and his family. *Tante* must have instructed the children on how to behave, for they came out the door quietly and joined us.

Then Chief Tsena spoke. "Pegasus ... *viene a mi tipi."*

I understood the words but not how Pegasus found his village.

"Como?" How? I asked.

He shrugged. *Quien sabe?"* Who knows? "Pegasus *muy inteligente."*

"Si, muy," I said. Very intelligent. *"Y usted muy bueno."* And you very good. I did not know the word for kind but I think he understood because he smiled.

"Porque su padre mi amigo por siempre," he answered.

Because your father my friend forever.

I nodded, remembering the painting Papa made of him.

"Su padre aqui?" Your father here?"

I shook my head. "No, no *hombres aqui. "Porque guerra."* Because war.

"Comprendo," the chief said. I understand. Then he motioned to our village with a sweeping gesture of his muscular arm. "Kiowa *viene aqui, toma caballos y mujeres y niños."*

Something about Kiowas, horses, women and children — maybe he means stealing them. A pang of alarm shot through my heart.

"Mucho cuidado," he went on. Much care.

I nodded and looked around at the women. "If you don't speak Spanish, Chief Tsena tells me that the Kiowas are stealing women and children as well as horses. And that we should be careful."

A collective gasp went up from the group.

"Donde?" someone asked. Where?

"Casa de campo por río," the chief said, pointing to the west. Farmhouse by river.

I was glad Mama was not here or she would start packing up to leave. And then a second thought came. Maybe that was a good idea. But not all the way to Germany.

Tante put her hand on my shoulder. "Thank him for the warning, Sophie, and tell him we are prepared."

I did not know how to say *prepared* so I said, *"Pistola,"* gun. *"Todas las mujeres tiene pistola."* All the women have gun. I removed mine from the holster and motioned for the others to do the same.

The chief looked around. *"Bueno."*

During all this, Nistiuma slid off his mother's horse, and Willie was teaching him to play pattycake. Though Nistiuma did not understand the words, they were having fun with the clapping game.

Chief Tsena looked down at them for a moment, grinning. "No *guerra!"* He clasped his hands together, his right covering his left. *"Paz."* He was making the sign for peace.

Then he handed me Pegasus' rope. *"Ahora tengo que ir. Adios."*

Anawakeo smiled, reached out her hand to Nistiuma. After one more clap with Willie, the boy took her hand and climbed up behind his mother. *"Adios,* Willie," he said.

Willie waved. *"Adios,* Nistiuma."

"Muchas gracias por Pegasus," I said, *"y por sus palabras."* I meant for your words of warning.

A chorus of *adios* came from the gathering as we waved farewell and watched them ride away. I don't think any of the women here will ever again assume that all Indians are hostile. But, as the chief said, some are. So we must be prepared.

Wednesday
November 9, 1864

I have been remiss about writing in this journal because nothing significant, either good or bad, has happened until today.

We had some good news! It spread rapidly over the telegraph lines. President Lincoln was reelected to a second term.

More good news. I received two letters from Eduard and will paste them here.

June 19, 1864

Liebe Sophie!

I hope you received my letter of April 12. Yours of May 1st came to me after four weeks, and I almost wish it never had. Or that you never had to witness such an awful deed. But awful deeds happen every day in war.

Please do not blame yourself. How could you go against all those violent men? They would think nothing of harming you if you had tried to save the man, and then they would have hanged him as well. I am thankful you had the instinct to flee and save yourself.

On a more pleasant note, there is a full moon rising as I write this letter. I want to think only of you instead of all the violence in the world. I hope you are watching the moon rise and thinking of me.

Yours,
Eduard

I was. Every full moon I think of Eduard and Papa. A full moon can be both terrible and beautiful. It was on such a night two years ago that Papa was wounded when Confederates ambushed his group as he and Eduard were on the way to Mexico to join the Union Army. Still, a full moon is beautiful when I think of Eduard and how he is thinking of me. It is almost as if we were watching it together.

Here is the second letter from him. Were there others in between?

October 15, 1864

Liebe Sophie,

No day passes without my thinking of you. I long to kiss you again and hold you in my arms. But for now I must keep myself safe so that I can return and do so.

As I have told you in another letter, I am with the Army of Tennessee, commanded by General Sherman. He is a good general if good means no mercy for the enemy, except for wounded and prisoners. He always says,"War is hell," and I agree.

Fortunately some of us soldiers now have a moment of rest. You may have read the news that Sherman took Atlanta. The mayor himself surrendered on September 2, and I have been here ever since.

I do see an end to this war and all the killing. Meanwhile, I keep the lines you gave me from *William Tell* close to my heart:

Whoever looks around with
open eyes

And trusts in God and his own
ready strength
Can keep himself from danger
and distress.

Yours,
Eduard

I imagined Eduard standing before me, so tall and manly, his blond hair falling across his forehead. He would look down at me with his blue eyes, tilt my chin up, and kiss my lips. I closed my eyes and remembered our first kiss, so light it made me yearn for more. But there were no more because he left for the war the next morning. I was only thirteen years old and, although Eduard was fifteen, he could pass for two years older.

I am glad he keeps William Tell's words close to his heart. I must remember them as well and stay safe for Eduard's and Papa's return. But there is something I don't understand. How can I trust in God if I don't know what God is?

Papa and I used to discuss the question without ever arriving at an answer, only some ideas. Papa said it is the great mystery. Sometimes we might get a glimpse of the mystery, of how we are all part of the same One. Is that God?

How I miss those talks with Papa. Sometimes he spoke in Latin and then taught me the words. Many people in Comfort know Latin. In fact, Texans call us "Latin Farmers."

We also talked about my future. He wants me to attend Ursuline Academy in San Antonio after the war, even though it is Catholic. I like the idea but now there is so much uncertainty.

One thing is certain though. I want to be a writer. Indeed I *am* a writer of this journal and some poems. I was named for a German novelist, Sophie von LaRoche. Papa's idea, because as he said, on the first day of my life I looked intently at everything.

Now as I write, the fire is burning down and the cold creeping in. It is late and tomorrow is a school day. So I must bank the fire and go to bed. Mama and the children are already asleep, Willie and Lena in the same bed, curled together for warmth. I wondered if Mama wished Papa were lying in bed beside her.

Wednesday
November 23, 1864

Today was mail day and, wonder of wonders, we received a letter from Papa! When Willie and I came home from school, we first stopped in at *Frau* Bremer's where she and Mama were peeling potatoes for supper, and Lena played on the floor with a spinning top.

Willie immediately dropped down on the floor to show her how to make it spin.

"Nein!" Lena yelled and grabbed it from him. "My top."

"I was just going to show you how to do it," Willie said, pouting.

Frau Bremer stood. "I think I have another one in the boys' room." And she went upstairs to get it.

While she was gone, Mama said, "Sophie, there is a letter from Papa on our dining table."

My heart leaped with joy. "Any good news?" I asked.

"Nein, but some good advice."

"Come on, Willie, let's go read it. You can show Lena how to spin the top later."

"Never!" he said and I chuckled as we left the Bremers' house.

It was a cold, clear day, so Mama had left a small fire burning in the fireplace. Willie and I sat on the bench side by side as I opened the envelope.

"Read, read!" he said, swinging his short little legs.

"Patience, Willie," I said even though I was just as eager to read Papa's letter.

I will leave room here and paste it in.

New York, New York
October 13, 1864

Liebe Elisabet, Sophie, Willie, and Lena!

Your letter of April 17 reached me at long last. I can only hope this letter will get through the blockade.

After reading about the deserter, I am more concerned for your safety than for mine. All of you must stay close to home. Do not go out to our place for any reason, not even to pick the garden. Surely *Frau* Bremer has enough in her garden. Just help her take care of it.

As for myself, *Harper's Weekly* has sent me to the Shenandoah Valley in Virginia, which General Sheridan of the Union Army is attempting to take. I grow weary of drawing men killing each other. But if Sheridan succeeds, I think this war will soon end and I will come home to you. I live for that day.

Yours,
Friedrich (Papa)

"So do I, Papa," I said.

"Me too," Willie said, snuggling closer.

Then he sat up and turned to me with worried eyes. "But what if one of those men he draws shot Papa?"

My heart sank. Hundreds of thousands of men had been killed in the war already. Even though Papa was not on the battlefield, he was close. It was possible. *Would* he live for that day? Would Eduard? And what must I say to

Willie?

"Sophie? What if?"

I lay the letter on the table and took his plump little hand in both of mine. "Willie, I don't know. I honestly don't know. But he is safer than the soldiers."

Willie shook his head. "That's not good enough."

I wrapped my arm around him and pulled him close. "That's the best I can do, *Liebchen.*"

After a moment of thought, he stood and said, "I wish I could stand next to Papa and shout, NO FIGHTING! Then all the soldiers would lay down their guns, salute me, and say, Yes sir, General Willie."

I laughed and saluted him. "I wish so too, Willie. I'll write that in our next letter to Papa."

Friday
December 16, 1864

One of the worst days of my life. I said that once before when I found Papa half dead on the Nueces River. How many more days like this must I endure until the war is over? According to Odysseus, many.

I write with shaking hand and make ink blots. Just remembering what happened sets my heart racing. So I will take some deep breaths and begin at the beginning.

Christmas is almost here but the Kiowas don't know about baby Jesus. Or that Christmas is supposed to be a time for peace on earth and goodwill to men. Neither do leaders of our country, it seems. The war goes on.

It happened at school during lunch. *Tante* and the older children sat at the dining table, while Willie and the little ones ate in the kitchen with *Frau* Murck. I took my lunch to the couch where Etta sat before a blazing fire.

"What do you have?" she asked.

I took off the lid and showed her the hardboiled egg, sliced sausage, a small apple, and two of *Frau* Bremer's oatmeal raisin cookies.

"Mmmm, I'll trade you for one of those cookies," Etta said. Would you like a piece of Mama's gingerbread?" She grinned her irresistible grin.

"Sure."

As we ate our lunch and watched the leaping flames of the fire, she said, "Have you had any more letters from your husband?"

I gave her a nudge with my elbow. "Oh stop it, you silly girl. You're just jealous."

She pretended to pout, her lower lip pushed out.

Ever since Eduard and I were cast as William Tell and his wife Hedwig in Schiller's play at school for a reading, she has teased me.

"And you're right," she said. "Now I'll never get a boyfriend. I'll just be an old maid."

"Well, what about Thomas? He likes you." I was teasing her.

"That big dumb bully? I'd rather kick him than kiss him."

"Then what about Franz Kettner?" I asked seriously.

She cocked her head to one side. "*Ja,* I like him but he didn't even say goodbye when he went off to the war."

I thought of my tender farewell with Eduard and felt sorry I had teased her.

"Anyway," Etta went on, "all our future husbands will probably die in some stupid battle on some stupid hill for no stupid reason!"

"Ach, Etta, don't say that!"

She looked at me with sad eyes. "I'm sorry, Sophie. I know how much you like Eduard."

"I'm sorry, too, for teasing you."

We hugged and then ate our lunch in silence and, for me, a sense of despair.

Suddenly Willie came running to me. "Snow, Sophie! It's snowing! Can I go outside?"

I looked out the window beside the fireplace. Tiny snowflakes swirled down, the first of the season.

Willie stood waiting for an answer.

"Have you finished your lunch?"

He nodded eagerly. Fortunately he had worn knickers and long stockings.

"Then put on your jacket and cap and I'll go with you."

"So will I," Etta said.

By this time all the children were clamoring to go out.

"If you finished your lunch, you may put on your coats and go with Sophie and Etta," *Tante* said.

One by one they followed us out.

There was not yet enough snow to make snowballs but the children ran about with mouths open, spreading their arms, and letting snow fall on their faces and tongues. And squealing. Snow never gets old, especially the first of the season. It makes me feel like a child again. I turned my face toward the sky and let the flakes fall on me, amidst the squealing.

After a time, *Tante* rang the bell. "Come, *Kinder,* time for naps and afternoon lessons."

But where was Willie? Nowhere to be seen. Could he have gone to the *Häuschen?* Or to the barn to see Pegasus?

"Are you coming, Sophie?" Etta called.

"Nein. I don't know where Willie is. Did he go back in?"

"I'll see." Etta hurried in while I ran to the *Häuschen* behind the Altgelts' house and knocked on the door. No answer. I opened it. No Willie.

"He's not in the house," Etta called.

My heart leaped in alarm. "Willie! Where are you?" I yelled.

No answer.

NNNNN-hhhhh.

Pegasus!

I ran across the yard to the barn, pulling out my pistol on the way. From the corner of my eye, I could see Etta following me. The doors stood open, and as I got closer I heard scuffling and saw shadowy shapes moving about. "Willie?"

A few feet from the doorway I stopped and stared, frozen.

A tall, muscular Indian stood inside, holding Willie with one hand over his mouth. Willie kicked his heels at the man's shins and struggled to get loose. Behind them a younger Indian held a rope tied to Pegasus who tossed his head, pulling back on the rope, his eyes showing white.

"Alemán!" I yelled, *"Alemán!"*

They ignored me, trying to control Willie and Pegasus, who were both putting up a good fight.

My heart hammered against my chest. My mind reeled. Etta and I were no match for the two of them, and my pistol was useless. I dared not point it at them and endanger Willie and Pegasus. Should I grab Willie and pull him away? *Think, Sophie, think. Don't let fear blind you.*

William Tell's words flashed in my mind. *Open your eyes, trust in your own strength.*

I looked at the man's hand on Willie's mouth and suddenly knew what to do. But Willie had to do it.

"Willie!"

He stopped kicking and looked at me, his eyes wild with fear.

"Bite his hand!"

Willie clamped both hands over the Indian's and bit.

"Aaaiiii," he yelled and let go of Willie, who dashed to me, grabbed my skirt, and hid himself in a fold.

Meanwhile, Pegasus did his part, rearing up, threatening his would-be captors with his hooves. Even though they both tried to hold onto the rope, he pulled away and galloped to us.

Without glancing at Willie, I took hold of the pistol with both hands, my arms stretched out like a triangle. I got my sights lined up on the bigger man's chest and cocked the hammer.

He stared at me in silence with a look of ... what?

Something like respect. For a moment nothing moved, not even Willie ... until the man clasped his hands together, his right covering his left. The sign for peace.

I gasped. Did he mean it? Was it a trick?

Think, Sophie, think. I could kill him with a little squeeze of the trigger. He was square in my sights ... but I didn't want to kill him, especially when he was making the peace sign. Nor was I going to let anything happen to Willie or me. I would kill him in an instant if he came toward us. So what to do? How do I end this? Pegasus snorted and stamped his hooves.

"Shoot him, Sophie," Etta whispered from behind me.

"No fighting," Willie said in a squeaky little voice that was on the edge of crying.

I just wanted the man and boy to go away and never come back but I didn't know the word in Spanish. So I yelled, "Go!" and made a motion with my pistol.

The man looked at me for a moment. Then he took the boy by the arm and the two stepped slowly to the far edge of the doorway, made the peace sign again, turned and ran toward the creek. We watched them cross the creek, mount their horse, and gallop away.

I put my pistol in the holster, knelt down, and hugged Willie. "All is well now, Willie. We are safe." Our hearts pounded against each other.

After a time he said, "I know," pulled away, and wiped his eyes with the back of his hand. "You kept me safe just like you always said."

"You saved yourself, Willie, with your sharp little teeth."

Willie grinned. *"Ja,* but he didn't taste so good!" He spit on the ground.

Etta and I laughed even though I felt shaky.

"But what were you doing in the barn?" I asked Willie.

"I just went in to see Peg and the Indian grabbed me."

"I can't believe he let you go and now we're laughing about it," Etta said. "What was that sign he made with his hands?"

"A peace sign."

"Do you think he meant it?"

"I don't know but with Willie's bite and my pistol pointed at him, he really had no choice."

"It was because I said no fighting."

"Or because I said shoot him," Etta said.

"I'm glad I did not need to do so."

"Sophie, Etta, Willie, what are you doing?" It was *Tante* standing outside the door of her house. "Time to come in."

"Coming," I said. Then turning to Willie, I said, "Go in with Etta. I'm going to put Pegasus back in his stall and lock the barn. Don't tell what happened until I come in."

Willie nodded.

I reached out to Pegasus who tossed his head and pranced to me. "Oh, Peg, you helped save our Willie and yourself." I stroked his silky white forehead. "If you were not so beautiful, they wouldn't try to steal you."

After leading him back to his stall in the barn, I locked the doors and brought the key to the house.

Everyone turned to me as I entered. The little ones lay on their mats for a nap but lifted their heads. The older students sat at the dining table with *Tante,* who stopped reading aloud.

Willie scrambled up. "Can I tell now, Sophie?"

"Tell what?" *Tante* asked.

"About the Indians who tried to steal me and Pegasus but I bit his hand and they both ran away!"

"And Sophie pulled her gun on them," Etta added.

Tante gasped and the children looked stunned. Then everyone started talking.

"Calm down, *Kinder,* and let Sophie tell us what happened." *Tante* said.

So I told the story, praising Willie's bravery and William Tell's words that gave me the courage to look around and not panic.

Afterward *Tante* said, "Well, I'm proud of you both and I will see that the barn door is always locked from now on." She turned to the other children then. "You must tell your mothers what happened. And I will put up a notice in Faltin's, warning all the women in the village."

When school was over for the day, *Tante* went out first with her pistol in hand to make sure those two Indians had not returned.

"All clear, *Kinder.* Now go straight home."

As Willie and I walked home with Etta, I told him to let me do the telling. He nodded, shaking his curly blond hair, but I was not convinced.

"Good luck, Sophie," Etta said as we left her at her house.

Mama was not in our cabin so we went to *Frau* Bremer's.

She and Mama were in the kitchen shelling peas for dinner. Lena played with some wooden blocks.

Willie rushed to Mama. "Guess what?"

"What, *Liebchen?*"

"Willie, *nein!*" I said.

He turned to me. "I was just going to say you have something to tell."

Mama looked at me with a question in her eyes.

I had been searching for the right words as we walked home but there were none.

"Mama ..." I hesitated.

She frowned.

"While we were at school an Indian tried to steal Pegasus."

"And me," Willie proudly announced.

"Willie, *bitte,* let me tell her."

He nodded.

"Fortunately I had Papa's pistol and made him leave us alone."

Mama stood abruptly. The pan banged on the floor and peas scattered everywhere. "You could have shot Willie!"

"Ach, Mama, you know I would never point a gun at him!"

"Nein, I don't know what you might do in a panic like that."

"I did not panic. I did what William Tell said."

"And what was that?"

"I kept my eyes open and trusted in my own strength."

She shook her head. "Sophie, this is too much. We're going back to Germany and live with your grandparents."

"But what about Papa? You know he can't go back." *And what about Eduard?* I thought but did not ask.

Frau Bremer set her pan aside and wiped her hands on her apron. "Elisabet, all of us women are facing danger and loss — facing it together."

Indeed, her two sons joined the Confederate Army rather than try to escape, and her husband hauls supplies for the army. It must be awful to fight for a cause you don't believe in.

Mama turned to her. "Our men *chose* to be in this war, Johanna, but when my children are threatened by savages ..." She put her face down in her hands.

Frau Bremer arose, stepped to Mama, careful to avoid the peas, and hugged her. Mama leaned her head on *Frau* Bremer's shoulder and let herself be comforted as if she were a daughter.

"Think carefully about such a decision," *Frau* Bremer went on. "The ports are blockaded. The only ships sailing in or out take a risk of being sunk by Union warships." She took Mama by the shoulders and looked into her eyes. "Truly, Elisabet, the risk of sailing is greater than the risk of staying."

For a moment there was silence while we waited for Mama to say something. She has always hated living on the frontier, beyond civilization, and often told Papa she wanted to leave. But she never threatened to do so.

With tears in her eyes, Mama nodded. "I know you are right, Johanna. Now is not a good time." She looked around at the peas on the floor. "I'm sorry for making such a mess."

"Well, I think we have plenty of hands to pick them up in no time."

Willie was already on his hands and knees doing so and putting them in the pan Mama dropped. Lena joined him as if it were a game. Some peas were mashed but we soon had the mess on the floor cleaned up ... if not the mess of our lives.

I did nothing, just stared at Mama, feeling fierce. And then I could hold back no longer.

"Do you mean you are going to leave when the blockade is lifted? No matter what?"

"Ja, I've had enough, Sophie."

"Well, I haven't. This is the only home I have ever known, the place where Papa will build our new house on the hill." I said nothing about Eduard but I thought it.

"And if he does *not* come home?"

Willie stood and put his little hand over Mama's mouth. *"Nein, nein,* Mama!"

I sat, stunned. What if her words made it come true? What if we were left alone? What would I do? Would I stay or go? Did I have a choice? I don't know. All I knew was that until this war is over, I had to keep our family safe. That is what Papa wanted me to do. I am the strong one, he said, so I must think how.

Was there some place nearby where we could go until the war ends? A place where hostile Indians and vigilantes did not go? A civilized place?

And then it came to me. San Antonio. Papa used to go there to sell his paintings and buy supplies. I have never been but if people buy paintings to hang on their walls, it must be civilized. And many Germans live in the city.

There was really no reason we had to stay in Comfort. Papa and Eduard were gone, and Arlis took care of our cattle and sheep. Most important, we would not have to be constantly on guard for hostile Indians or vigilantes.

All good. Still, where would we live? I decided to ask *Tante.* She has traveled to the city several times with her husband.

Meanwhile, we must make Christmas happen – for the children.

Christmas Eve, 1864

It is late but I want to write while all is still fresh in my mind and while Mama and the children are sleeping. I have a warm fire burning in the fireplace, thanks to Arlis for keeping us supplied with wood. Outside the waning moon rises over the snow-covered land. There is a deep silence with only the occasional popping of the fire and the scratching of my pen.

Christmas was as good as *Frau* Bremer, Mama, and I could make it in the absence of the men in our two families. For the moment, Mama seemed to forget about returning to Germany. And in the busyness of preparations, I had little time to think about the war.

Yesterday afternoon Arlis brought firewood and a cedar tree. Snow was beginning to fall as he stacked the wood on *Frau* Bremer's gallery and ours. Willie and I helped him. Arlis may be in his sixties with white hair and beard, but he is still strong.

Then he set up the tree in her living room. Mama paid him in silver coins, and *Frau* Bremer gave him sausage and potato salad to take home. I had made ginger cookies to hang on the tree and gave him some of those.

"Fröhliche Weihnachten, Arlis," I said. Merry Christmas.

He dipped his head in thanks. *"Danke, liebe Damen,"* dear ladies.

"We could not manage without you, Arlis," Mama said.

His face twisted into a lopsided smile. "I know that, *Frau* Guenther. I do it with pleasure." He dipped his head, put on his hat, and left.

As snow continued to fall I watched him walk away beside the oxen pulling our wagon. It made me sad to think of his spending Christmas alone in his little cabin. Still, I knew he would be uncomfortable spending it with us. He lived alone out in the country and seemed to prefer it that way.

This afternoon Willie and I made a snowpapa, Willie's word, just outside the front gate of *Frau* Bremer's garden. There was plenty of snow, more snow at Christmas than I have ever seen, probably a foot deep. We rolled three balls of snow, big, medium, and small, and set them one on top of the other.

"Look for some rocks for his eyes, Willie, while I go inside and see if there is a hat we can borrow."

Digging in the snow, Willie found two round brown rocks for Papa's eyes, and *Frau* Bremer loaned me one of her husband's hats, a black one that reminded me of Papa. Then I added some snow and shaped his nose, and Willie added a smiling row of pebbles for his mouth. For arms we found tree branches and stuck them in the sides of his body.

"Papa looks like he is about to wrap his arms around me," Willie said.

"And one day he will," I told him, although I was not sure.

Tonight Willie and Lena stayed in *Frau* Bremer's kitchen as she and Mama prepared supper and I decorated the tree in the living room. The door between us was closed so that the children could not see the tree until the *Weihnachtsmann* came. That is what we call Santa Claus.

Frau Bremer had set out a box of tree decorations. There was even a glass strawberry like one we used to have before I dropped it. She also had made popcorn, which I threaded into a garland with cranberries and draped it around the tree. After hanging the ginger cookies, I clamped the candleholders onto branches and put the gifts under the tree. There were woolen caps knitted by Mama. *Frau* Bremer made a ragdoll for Lena and gave Willie a wooden ball and cup toy that belonged to one of her sons. And there were even some oranges and apples.

When all was ready, we had supper in the kitchen. As usual, Willie squirmed about in his chair, too excited to eat.

"Remember what your papa said," Mama reminded him. "The *Weihnachtsmann* does not come until the children finish their dinner."

"I remember." Willie took a bite of sausage. "You too, Lena."

She looked at him and then scooped up some potato salad with her spoon. "See? I eat."

When we finished supper, I said, "I'll go and see if he has come. No peeking now."

I opened the door to the living room and closed it behind me. After lighting the candles and making sure everything was in place, I opened the door.

"The *Weihnachtsmann* has come, *Kinder.*"

Willie slid off his chair and took Lena by the hand. "Come on, Lena, let's see what he left for us."

The tree glowed with glass ornaments sparkling in the candlelight, and cookies hung waiting to be plucked and eaten. Willie and Lena stood side by side, holding hands, their faces glowing with excitement.

Then, looking at Mama, Willie remembered. "But first we sing."

Mama smiled and sat down at the piano in the far corner of the room. Lena crawled up on the bench beside her and Willie stood at her side. She played as we sang.

O Tannenbaum, O Tannenbaum,
How faithful are your branches.
Not only green in summertime,
But also in freezing wintertime...

It brought tears to my eyes, remembering Papa's deep voice that was missing tonight.

Mama played two more verses while I remembered Christmas four years ago, the year the war started. Papa came home on Christmas Eve from a trip to San Antonio to sell his paintings. It was snowing that night too, and I helped him unload the wagon in the barn. On the way home he had seen a burned cabin and the owner hanging from a tree out front. Hanged for being a Unionist.

Well, that scared me.

I begged him not to draw any more cartoons because those vigilantes might come for him.

I can remember what Papa said then, word for word. He said, "There are worse things than death, Sophie."

What? I wanted to know. Nothing could be worse.

"Not being true to oneself," he said.

I told him I didn't care about that. I didn't want anything to change or die.

He said, "Sophie, everything does change whether you want it to or not. Everything that is alive grows and changes."

"And dies!" I shouted.

Now I feared my words could come true for Papa or Eduard.

Suddenly I was brought back to the present by the children's squealing. Willie and Lena ran to the tree that stood beside the fireplace. He handed her the ragdoll. She cuddled it and said, *"Püppchen,"* little doll.

"Ja, Lena," *Frau* Bremer said. "Is that what you want to name her?"

Lena nodded and so it was.

Willie understood his ball and cup toy right away. The red ball was attached to the handle by a string and the idea was to toss and catch the ball in the cup. He tossed the ball and tried to catch it, time after time.

"This is hard, Sophie. Can you do it?"

I tried several times but the ball just bounced off the cup. I handed it back to Willie because I wanted him to do it first. "It's your toy, Willie, so keep on practicing."

When he caught the ball at last, we all applauded him as he paraded around the room to show everyone. "I did it, I did it!" he said with a big grin that made dimples in his cheeks, just like Papa's.

Outside a cold wind blew snow against the windows but we were warm and safe inside the Bremers' house for now. Where were Papa and Eduard? Were they warm and safe? Were they thinking of us? Surely there is no fighting on Christmas Eve. Is there?

Wednesday
January 4, 1865

A new year and an old war. What will it bring, I wonder. Will it bring peace at last? We all grow weary of the war and so do the soldiers. More and more are deserting, more than Waldrip's Wolfpack can catch and hang.

Much to my delight, it brought a letter from Eduard. When Willie and I got home from school today, the letter waited for me on the plank table! I gasped for joy and opened it carefully with shaking hands.

I will paste it here in my journal so I can read it over and over.

December 4, 1864

Liebe Sophie,

May this letter find you and your family safe and well. No day passes without my thinking of you.

We have left Atlanta a burning ruin. Such a waste! General Sherman was determined to leave nothing behind that the Confederates could use.

Now we are on a march of destruction to Savannah. We forage for food we need and burn the rest. To his credit, Sherman ordered us not to enter any dwellings unless the inhabitants are hostile.

Sometimes I wonder why I was so eager to enlist and fight. You were right to question my intentions, yet what choice did I have? Only two. Fight for the Union to abolish slavery. Or fight for the Confederacy to save slavery. I like to think I am risking my life for a noble cause.

But there is one thing I never doubt. Through all this chaos and horror, what keeps me sane is the thought of you and returning to Comfort.

I first fell in love with you that day at school when *Herr* Steves announced that we were going to read aloud from *William Tell.* He assigned me to be Tell and you to be my wife, Hedwig. As we read, I looked at you, then you at me, and something passed between us, something prophetic.

If you feel the same way, cling to the idea with all your strength and one day we will see each other again.

Yours,
Eduard

Something prophetic. Oh, my heart! I *do* feel the same way. Now that I have written in my journal, I shall write a letter telling him so and begging him to keep himself from danger. I will promise to keep myself safe as well, and one day we will see each other again.

As part of that promise, tomorrow after school I will ask *Tante* about moving to San Antonio.

Thursday
January 5, 1865

Outside, snow lay on the ground, on roofs, and on branches. This is the coldest winter with more snow than anyone can remember. I wonder if it is the same for Papa and Eduard and hope the snow is so deep that there is no fighting. But do they have a fire to keep them warm?

When school was over, Etta and I stood warming ourselves before the fire. She bounced on her toes as she does when ready to go.

"You go on without Willie and me, Etta, because I need to talk with *Tante.*"

She put her hands on her hips and tilted her head to one side, her red hair seeming to radiate in the light of the fire. "About what?"

"I'll tell you later."

She pouted. "But we're best friends. You can tell me anything."

"I will … but later. Please, Etta."

"Promise?"

"*Ja,* I promise."

After everyone left except for Willie and me, I asked *Tante* if we could talk about something. Willie sat at the kitchen table with George and the other Altgelt children under the eye of *Frau* Murck, who fed them cookies and warm apple cider.

"Of course," *Tante* said, and motioned me to the couch before the fire.

"So, I'm listening," she said with a smile, settling her girlish figure onto the couch and arranging her blue calico skirts.

I nodded and began. "I have not told Mama yet because I wanted to see what you think about ..." I hesitated. It seemed like such a rash decision to make.

She studied me with her dark, hooded eyes.

"Ja? Go on, Sophie. I'm not going to be shocked."

"About our family moving to San Antonio."

Tante drew a breath and took my hand. "Well, *meine Liebe,* I would miss your family but I think it is just what Elisabet needs, a safe, civilized place until your papa comes home. I, too, would leave Comfort except for the fact that Ernst founded it, and I don't want to abandon all these women."

"That's a good reason but you are stronger than Mama."

Tante smiled. "Don't forget that I am a soldier's daughter. He taught me how to take care of myself."

"Ja, I remember. But Mama told me her father ruled the family like a tyrant and gave women no credit for saving themselves."

"What a pity."

"So Papa calls me the strong one, and I'm trying to live up to his words. The problem is where would we live?"

Tante thought a moment and then sat forward. "Sophie, I have an idea. I know the Mengers who own a hotel on Alamo Plaza, a splendid place. They are German too. I read in the newspaper that they shut down the guest rooms until the war is over for lack of help but I feel sure you could stay there. Mary Menger is an unpretentious lady, a real German *Hausfrau.* She amazes me. For all her wealth and position as owner, she goes to the market herself and is a gourmet cook. Perhaps Elisabet could assist her in the kitchen in return for your stay."

"Ja, I think she would."

Tante leaned back with a satisfied expression on her face. "I'll write Mary a letter this very day."

In a moment she went on. "As for school, I can loan you the first volume of Gibbon's history of Rome. That should keep you busy. And you can take some McGuffey Readers for Willie. Also remember, if you are still there next fall, there is Ursuline Academy."

"That's where Papa wanted me to go!"

She nodded. *"Ja,* for good reason. It is an excellent school, even if Catholic. Those nuns are very dedicated to a good education for young women like you, Sophie. You should apply to be a student. And I'll send them a letter of recommendation."

"Thank you, *Tante,* I will. I just hope Mama likes the idea."

Still, I thought, it would be sad to leave Etta. I even felt a little guilty for liking the idea of leaving. I dreaded her reaction. Of course I would say nothing until *Tante* received an answer from *Frau* Menger — no matter how much she begged.

Wednesday
February 15, 1865

Today our lives changed, as you will see, dear Reader!

After school I sat in one of the armchairs reading the *San Antonio Zeitung* that came in the mail today. Mama sat in the other, knitting socks before a warm fire. Willie and Lena were at *Frau* Bremer's house. She loved having them visit and play with her sons' old toys.

News of the war was good for the Union if you call destruction good. General Sherman's army, which Eduard is part of, left Savannah and was marching through South Carolina, destroying everything in their path with a fury never shown before. Sherman is quoted as saying, "The devil himself could not restrain my men in that state." Maybe because it was the first state to secede and start the war.

I knew what Eduard thought of all that destruction. At least it was property not people. Did he have to join in? Will he be a different man when he returns? As I pondered, someone tapped on the door.

I lay the paper aside and took Papa's pistol from a high bookshelf, clutching it in the folds of my long skirts, and stepped to the door.

"Who is it?"

"Emma Altgelt," came the answer.

I opened the door. "What a nice surprise, *Tante,* come in."

She stomped the snow from her laced-up boots and glanced at the gun at my side. "I'm glad to see you are prepared, Sophie."

"Emma!" Mama stood. "How good to see you."

Tante removed her cape and silk bonnet and shook the snow onto the hearth. "Well, I had to get out of the house so I braved the cold." She smoothed her dark hair back to the bun atop her head. "Besides, I have some good news."

A thrill passed through me. It must be about the Menger Hotel. I had told Mama nothing.

"Is the war over?" Mama asked in jest. "Come, sit here, Emma, and warm yourself while I brew some hot coffee for us." She always kept a pot of hot water hanging on a hook in the fireplace. "Then you can tell us your good news."

After putting the pistol back on the top shelf, I settled myself on the rug in front of the two armchairs, my back to the fire. I could hardly wait to hear what *Tante* had to say. She looked at me, smiled and nodded but said nothing until Mama set the coffee cups on the table between the chairs and sat down.

"So, Elisabet, are you ready to move to San Antonio?" *Tante* asked.

Mama looked astounded and put her cup back in the saucer so suddenly that her coffee sloshed. "What? What are you talking about, Emma?"

"*Ach,* Sophie, you didn't tell your mother?"

"*Nein,* I didn't want her to be disappointed if nothing happened."

"Disappointed about what?"

"Let me explain then, Elisabet," *Tante* said. "Your daughter, thinking of your family's safety, asked me about moving to San Antonio. It so happens that I know the owners of the Menger Hotel there and wrote a letter to Mary Menger, the wife, to see if you could possibly stay there until the war is over. Today I had a letter from her."

She paused, seeming to enjoy the suspense.

"Your family is welcome to come live at the hotel at no cost until the war ends. And they have a stable for Pegasus."

I gasped and put my hand over my heart. So it was really going to happen!

"Mary says the stagecoach stops at the hotel front door." *Tante* looked at me with her keen brown eyes, the corners of her small mouth turned up.

I kept quiet, letting the two women discuss the matter.

"I don't know what to say, Emma," Mama said at last.

"Well, are you glad?" *Tante* asked.

"I am excited and fearful at the same time."

"Fearful of what? That is the reason for going, to avoid living in fear."

"Travel and so many strangers."

"Come now, Elisabet, be bold! Mary Menger knows everyone in San Antonio and she is so friendly. She told me that she once bought a painting from your Friedrich called *Cypress Cathedral.*"

I gasped, remembering when Papa came home from a trip to San Antonio, and said he had sold two paintings. Who could have imagined that four years later we would live in the owner's hotel?

"Also," she went on, "it is a perfect opportunity for Sophie to look at Ursuline Academy for the future."

Mama frowned. "But what will we eat? We'll have no garden, no meat, no stove for cooking. All I have is some Mexican silver from Arlis selling beef."

"Liebe Elisabet," *Tante* said, "trust me, Mary is not going to let you starve. Pay what you can and volunteer to help out in the kitchen."

And so it was decided. Mama would ask Arlis to drive us to Sisterdale in the wagon, and there we would take a stagecoach to San Antonio. Since I did not want to leave Pegasus for fear the Indians would steal him, I would ride him. After all, two years ago I had ridden him out to the Nueces River to look for Papa, and that was twice as far.

But first I had to tell Etta and I dreaded her reaction. I imagined her screaming, *Nein, nein, nein, Sophie! You can't do that to me,* wagging her head back and forth, as her red braids flew.

Thursday
February 16, 1865

As Etta, Willie, and I walked home from school today, she frolicked, dancing around Willie, which inspired him to hop about on his stubby little legs. It was a sunny, crisp day, such a relief from all the snow. And it was time to tell Etta about moving, much as I dreaded it.

"Etta, remember when I stayed after school to talk to *Tante* and you wanted to know why and I promised to tell you later?"

She stopped her dancing. *"Ja,* why? Tell me."

"Do you promise to remain calm?"

"Gut or bad?"

Willie said, "We're ..."

I held up my hand to stop him. "Both."

"I'll try, Sophie."

I paused for a moment, gazing at her freckled face and frizzy red hair that could barely be held in place by braids.

Then I said the words fast to get them out. "We are moving to San Antonio until the war is over and the men come home."

Etta's mouth fell open in disbelief.

"NEIN!" She put her hands on her hips.

"Etta, you promised," I reminded her.

"But why?"

"I think you know that my mother is worried after what happened to Willie."

"Well then, your mother and the little ones could go and you could stay here and live with us. My mother would love it. We could be sisters."

Willie ran to me and wrapped his arms around my waist. "*NEIN!*"

I shook my head. "*Danke,* Etta, that would be lovely but my mother would never allow it. And neither would Willie. Anyway, I won't be gone forever – just 'til the war is over and the men come home."

Etta frowned. "If it ever is — maybe when everybody kills everybody else."

"NO FIGHTING," Willie screamed. "My papa is coming home – he said so."

"It's all right, Willie." I patted his head and turned to Etta.

"Don't say that. You're talking about our fathers."

"And your future husband."

I smiled. "Perhaps."

Then Etta came and wrapped her arms around both of us. "I'm sorry, Sophie and Willie."

We hugged for a moment in silence and let go.

"I'll miss you, Etta. You're my best friend."

"And you are mine, Sophie, forever."

Wednesday

The Ides of March

If Papa were here he would read from Shakespeare's *Julius Caesar,* the part when Caesar ignores the soothsayer's warning, "Beware the Ides of March," and is assassinated in the Roman Forum on this day.

Instead, on this Ides of March we left Comfort by the light of a waning gibbous moon hanging in the west. There was no soothsayer's warning but maybe there should have been. There was only *Frau* Bremer, *Tante,* and Etta to say goodbye. *Tante* had brought Pegasus, and Arlis waited beside the oxen hitched to our wagon.

"It will be lonely without you," *Frau* Bremer said, hugging each of us in turn.

"We will miss you too, Johanna, and *danke* for taking us in," Mama said.

"And I'll take you back whenever you return," she replied.

I wondered to myself when that might be. When would Papa and Eduard come home?

"Did you remember to pack Gibbon's history of Rome?" *Tante* asked me.

"Ja, and Willie's books too," I said.

"Zehr gut. I will miss our book talks, Sophie. And I hope you will continue to keep a journal and write poems.

If so, send me one."

"And me, too," Etta said, "but I'll never forgive you for leaving me all alone." She gave me a fierce hug as if not to let me go.

"We'll be back, Etta, and I promise to write."

"Time to go, *Damen*," Arlis said.

Mama lifted Lena into the front of the wagon and Willie clambered up using the wooden wheel spokes. Then Arlis helped Mama climb in and I mounted Pegasus. *Frau* Bremer had loaned me her younger son's knickerbockers to wear under my skirt since I would never use the sidesaddle for such a distance.

"Step up!" Arlis commanded the oxen and gave them a prod with his stick as he walked along beside them. I gave Pegasus a nudge with my heels and we were off.

I turned one last time to wave. The three stood close together, silhouetted by the moonlight. I felt two ways: guilty for leaving them in a village without men while we ran to safety, and excitement about living in San Antonio, a big city.

We moved along in silence, each with our own thoughts, or for Willie and Lena, dreams. The two of them lay down on blankets to finish their interrupted night's sleep. The moon slowly sank as we made our way along the road that follows the broad Guadalupe River Valley. I rode Pegasus on one side of the oxen and Arlis walked on the other. He always kept the wheels oiled so the wagon rolled along the dirt road quietly.

Tree frogs warbled back and forth down by the river, and a night bird called *poor-will, poor-will.* A little shiver passed through my body. What would the coming day bring?

Gradually the sky grew pink. A few clouds gathered around, drawn to the sun as it peeked over the horizon. All this time I had been pondering what San Antonio would be like. I had never been to a big city. Comfort and Sisterdale were all I knew of the world except for the wilderness on the way to the Nueces River.

I remembered Papa's painting of Dresden, Germany, that he did as a student at the Academy of Fine Arts there. It showed an elegant stone bridge of multiple archways across the Elbe River where a great cathedral rose above the banks. Would San Antonio be so grand?

We arrived in Sisterdale midmorning. It is a community of scattered farms within walking distance of each other. At the center stand the general store and a stone schoolhouse. Since Papa and Mama had friends here, we used to visit now and then. Like Comfort, it is another settlement of Freethinkers and Latin Farmers but now the men had all gone.

At the store I dismounted and Arlis led Pegasus to a water trough. The children climbed out of the wagon, and Mama followed bringing some bread and cheese that *Frau* Bremer had wrapped for us.

"I'm hungry," Willie said.

"Me too." Lena followed Mama to the gallery where tables and chairs were set up for customers.

I took Willie and Lena to the *Häuschen* while Mama entered the store. She knew the wife of the owner, and the two of them returned with a pitcher of water and a tray of glasses.

Frau Hoffman, a slim dark-haired woman, said, "Ah, Sophie, you're all grown up now, a young lady. And look at you, Willie."

"*Ja,* I'm a young man."

"And this one I've not seen before." She meant Lena, who pulled away.

"Well, I surely hope life in San Antonio suits you. If I could I would go myself."

Around noon the stagecoach arrived, pulled by four black horses. It was quite elegant, painted bright red with yellow spoke wheels, a canvas top, and open windows. The driver helped the passengers step out, a middle-aged woman, a young boy, and an older man, her father as it turned out. Meanwhile, the driver and guard unhitched the horses, led them away, and brought fresh ones. As they were being hitched, Arlis loaded our bags into the boot, a compartment at the rear of the stagecoach. "Have a safe journey and don't worry about your homeplace. It's in good hands."

"*Danke,* Arlis," Mama said. "Friedrich would appreciate your care."

He nodded, reached out and shook Willie's hand as if he were a man, then looked at me. "*Fräulein* Sophie, never doubt that you did all that was possible for the deserter."

I smiled at his thoughtfulness. "I could not have done it without your help, Arlis."

When the mailbag had been loaded under the driver's seat, the guard opened the door and assisted the passengers into the coach. Willie insisted on helping himself and the guard complied with a knowing smile. When I mounted Pegasus, the driver stepped up to me. He was a big man with a wide-brimmed hat.

"Little lady, you keep close beside us on that fine

horse of yours. I don't want to leave you behind, so let me know if you need to slow down. We'll be making a stop in Boerne, thirteen miles from here."

I dipped my head and thanked him. What a gentleman. I had not expected him to be so thoughtful, judging by his rugged looks. Maybe a man that strong can let himself be gentle and caring.

And so we were off at a trot. The guard sat beside the driver, his double-barreled shotgun in hand. Willie stood at the window on my side of the coach, waving to me and grinning. It was a great adventure for him, and I caught his spirit. Soon we reached a shallow fording place on the Guadalupe River where giant cypress trees grew at the edge like church columns. We splashed across and up the gently sloping bank.

"Indians on the left," the guard shouted.

Downstream a distance, four Indians driving a small herd of horses galloped toward us. My heart leaped into pounding. I was on the same side of the stagecoach as the Indians. Would they come take Pegasus and me too?"

"Alemán!" I shouted.

"Let's go, little lady!" the driver yelled. He lashed the horses with his whip. I gave Pegasus a kick with my heels, and we raced on down the road. The guard leveled his shotgun at them. I pulled my pistol from the holster but did not cock it – not yet.

"Don't shoot unless they come after us," the guard yelled. "We're not here to save horses."

"Alemán! No fighting!" Willie screamed in his high-pitched voice.

I kept even with the stagecoach and looked back once. To my great relief the Indians continued on their course along the river. They must have decided that a herd of horses was more important than a Spirit Horse. Or maybe shouting *Alemán* kept them from pursuing us.

Gradually we slowed our pace to a fast walk, as did my heart. Pegasus could have kept on but the mules seemed relieved, snorting and blowing. I put my pistol back in the holster and pulled slightly on the reins to stay beside the stagecoach.

Willie stood at the door window. "We did it, Sophie!"

I smiled at him but my lips felt a little trembly.

The other boy leaned out the back window, watching the Indians and their herd. Mama sat, her hand covering her mouth as if to keep from screaming. Once we were out of sight, she leaned back, cradling Lena.

We continued through rolling hills and came to Boerne around noon. We entered the wide main street planted with trees on both sides and stopped at the general store. There were a few wagons and carriages up and down the street. Women and children clustered on galleries and crossed from one side to the other. I dismounted and led Pegasus to a water trough beside the store and then tied him to a railing along with some other horses. The passengers gathered on the gallery to talk about the encounter with the Indians.

"This convinces me that we're doing the right thing, Sophie," Mama said. "I've had enough of those savages. I never want to see another one."

"Ja, I agree," the other woman said.

I bit my lips together, thinking, *They are not all savages.* But I did not want to get into an argument that would change no one's mind.

Willie stretched up his arms to me. "Can I ride with

you, Sophie? *Bitte?*"

"Nein, Willie. It's too long a trip and you're getting so big."

After we all made a trip to the *Häuschen*, the driver said, "All aboard that's comin' aboard," and helped the passengers back into the stagecoach. I mounted Pegasus.

When the driver took his seat, he turned to me and said, "You done good, little lady."

I thanked him.

"I don't think we'll see any more Indians 'til we get to the city," he went on. "But they're friendly."

That was good news, and I repeated it to Mama and the other passengers.

And so we started off again. The road gradually descended out of the hill country onto a mesquite plain and finally to San Antonio. The sun hung halfway down the sky, shining on the adobe houses on the outskirts. As we entered the city, these houses gave way to stone mansions with front porches and balconies decorated by wooden latticework. We rode past them toward the center on a street filled with wagons and buggies and pedestrians of all kinds, Texan, German, Mexican, Negro, and yes, even a few Indians. It was a city such as I had never seen, only dreamed about.

We crossed a wooden bridge, came to a plaza, and pulled up in front of an elegant two-story stone hotel, the Menger. The arched windows on the second floor balcony glittered with light from the setting sun. People strolled about the plaza or sat on benches. Music and laughter spilled out of buildings across the plaza.

This was the last stop for the stagecoach. The driver and guard climbed down, helped the passengers alight, and unloaded baggage from the boot. I dismounted and stood beside Pegasus.

Holding Lena by the hand, Mama stepped up on the stone sidewalk and gazed at the hotel. On either side of the paneled front door, the tall windows shone with the light of gas lamps, welcoming us.

"Oh, it's almost like being in Dresden with its elegant buildings!" Mama said.

Willie ran to me. "Is this our new house?"

"You might say so, Willie, at least for a while."

He jumped up and down and clapped his hands. "I like it."

A carriage arrived for the other passengers, and we said *auf Wiedersehen* and *viel Glück*.

The guard came to me then. "I'll take your fine friend to the hotel stable, where he'll be well cared for."

I gave Pegasus a hug and wished him *gute Nacht.*

The driver then climbed up on his seat. "It was a pleasure to bring you people here safely." He saluted us. "*Adios,* as they say in San Antonio."

"I'm going to be a stagecoach driver when I grow up," Willie announced.

"You bet, young man," the driver called back as he drove away.

"Wait here with Willie," Mama told me. "I'll go and get help." With Lena in tow, she entered the front door.

She soon returned with a stocky little man who had a fringe beard along his jaw and chin. It was William Menger himself, with a boy who looked a couple of years younger than me.

"Herzlich Willkommen," the man said, smiling.

His welcome warmed my heart. Though I had never

performed a curtsy, I was inspired to do so.

Herr Menger bowed in response. "You must be Sophie. I have heard much about you from Emma Altgelt. And you, young man, must be William, like me."

"*Ja,* but I'm called Willie. And this is my little sister Lena."

Herr Menger nodded and gestured to the boy at his side. "And meet my son Louis."

They picked up our baggage and *Herr* Menger said, "Now come with us and we will get you settled in your new home. And my Mary has invited you to dine with us this evening."

"How lovely," Mama said.

We followed them into the lobby. I caught my breath. It was a soaring two-story space with a balcony around the second floor and a wrought iron balustrade. White columns with golden capitals reached up to the ceiling, and gas lamps on the walls lit the space. And there, on the wall to the left, hung Papa's painting, *Cypress Cathedral.*

"Mama, look!" I said. "It's Papa's painting. Remember when he came home from San Antonio at Christmas and said he sold two paintings and this was one of them?"

Mama put her hand over her heart and gasped. "*Ja,* Sophie, I *do* remember." She turned to *Herr* Menger. "Thank you for purchasing this painting, *Herr* Menger, especially since all his others were destroyed when our house was set on fire."

"*Ach,* dear lady, I am sorry to hear that. Hopefully, this war will soon be over and he can take up his brush again." He nodded once as if to make it so. "Actually, it was my wife who bought the painting from your husband,

and she would be here to greet you but she and her cook are in the kitchen preparing supper. We have some Confederate officers to feed as well." Then as an aside he said, "It never hurts to accommodate those in charge, no matter which side you support."

With a wave of his arm he gestured for us to come to the front counter. There he opened the guestbook. "Mary and I are very proud of our guestbook with its notable signatures, including Sam Houston. So now please add yours."

Mama signed for her and Lena. I lifted Willie up so he could print his name, and then I signed. Turning back the pages, I noticed Sam Houston wrote, "Sam Houston and horse." I laughed and added, "and Pegasus" after my name.

But I must stop writing, dear Reader. It has been a long day and I am exhausted. Tomorrow I will write about dinner with the Mengers and an encounter with a Confederate officer.

Now I sit at a desk in our parlor on the second floor, writing by the light of a pair of oil lamps. One has a figure of a girl in brass, balancing the oil font on her head. The other is a young man holding the font on his broad shoulders. I'm pretending one is me and the other is Eduard.

Mama, Willie, and Lena are already sound asleep in our bedroom. So I will turn down the wick and blow out the flame, first on my lamp and then Eduard's. Will I ever see him again?

Thursday
March 16, 1865

Now about last night's dinner. As we entered the spacious Colonial Dining Room, *Herr* Menger stood and motioned us to their oval table beside a window. The room was almost empty except for three other tables, occupied by Confederate officers in their gray uniforms. Even though I knew the Mengers were providing meals for officers, I gasped at the sight.

"Do they know we're enemies?" Willie whispered.

"Nein, don't say anything. We mustn't let them know."

I wanted to avoid them, pretend not to see them, but we had to pass by one of their tables to get to the Mengers. I took Willie's hand. Mama, holding Lena's hand, walked on without a glance, but Willie stared at them. One of the officers grinned and gave him a smart salute.

"Greetings, young man."

Willie stopped and looked up at me with a question in his eyes.

I wondered at the officer's friendliness. Perhaps he had a son Willie's age. He was the enemy, fighting for slavery, but he seemed like a decent human being.

I nodded to Willie and he saluted back.

"No fighting," Willie said in his small high voice.

It warmed my heart and I think I even smiled.

The officers laughed but the saluting one said, "Good

advice, young man. I'll pass that along to General Lee."

Suddenly I was filled with hope that soldiers were tired of killing each other and would throw down their arms and go home. Still, one side had to win and one side had to lose. If the South won, would we still have slavery? Much as I hate slavery, I hate war more.

As we walked on to the Mengers' table, *Frau* Menger rose. She is a smiling, plump lady with her dark hair parted in the middle and pulled back into a coiled braid.

"*Willkommen.* I am *Frau* Menger." She embraced Mama. "Call me Mary, and may I call you Elisabet?"

Mama smiled. "Of course, Mary."

Then she hugged me to her ample breast. "Sophie, I assume."

"*Ja, Frau* Menger." She made me feel as if we had been friends for a long time.

"And you must be Willie," she said.

"*Ja,*" Willie said, "and this is my little sister Lena. I am six years old and she is three."

Lena hid behind Mama's skirts.

"And I think you are a little gentleman," *Frau* Menger said.

I saw Willie clamp his lips together to keep from objecting to *little.*

"Now," she continued, "please meet my children. Louis William, whom you already know and who shares your name, Willie, though we call him Louis. He is thirteen, which I can hardly believe." She shook her head.

Louis, a tall slender youth, stood like a gentleman, nodded and smiled.

"Next comes Peter, who is eight years old." *Frau*

Menger gestured to the shy-looking little boy. "And last our youngest, Catherine Barbara, whom we call Babette and so may you. She is five."

Babette sat between her brothers. She wiggled as she was being introduced, making her dark curls bounce. As the only girl, Babette seemed to know she was the family favorite.

"Now, please be seated," *Frau* Menger said.

Herr Menger held our chairs, and we settled ourselves at the table.

"It is our pleasure to have your family here, Elisabet," *Frau* Menger went on. "Our hotel has not been busy during the war, except, as you can see, some Confederate officers. We also have a few rooms being used for wounded soldiers, who are being treated here." Glancing at me, she said, "I'm sure the nurses would be glad for any help you could give, Sophie, like reading books aloud or writing letters."

I nodded my willingness, even though it was a strange thought — helping soldiers who might have been wounded while fighting against Eduard. Still, it was something I could do to earn our keep.

Those thoughts were swept aside as the kitchen servants began bringing bowls of soup.

"It's turtle soup, a specialty of mine," *Frau* Menger said. "Made from turtles here in the San Antonio River."

Next came cold cuts and vegetables, served with rye bread, cheeses, wine, and spring water for the little ones.

"My wife is known for her cooking and her care in purchasing the finest fruit and vegetables available," *Herr*

Menger said. "That's why I married her!"

We laughed but I suspected it was partly true, especially since she was older than he. And she had a motherly way about her.

"This is delicious, Mary," Mama said. "We are so fortunate to be in a safe place with good food to eat. I am eager to earn our keep. How can I help you in the kitchen?"

"Danke, Elisabet. Once you are settled in, come down to the kitchen and we can work together. Of course, I have a cook but you and I can peel potatoes and shell peas together in the patio."

This made me like her even more. Wealthy as they must be to build this fine hotel, she is still a simple *Hausfrau,* like *Tante* said.

As we dined, *Frau* Menger turned to me. "Emma Altgelt wrote me about your desire to attend Ursuline Academy, Sophie."

I nodded. "It is my dream and my father's too."

"Then I will send a note to Sister St. Marie, the Mother Superior, and request an appointment for an interview."

Interview? Would she ask me if I was a Freethinker? Did she know that Freethinkers do not read the Bible *or go to church?*

Frau Menger went on. "The school is just a short walk or horseback ride from here. Our Babette will attend in the fall."

Babette grinned. "I'm going to ride my horse."

Frau Menger turned to her husband. "Perhaps you could escort Sophie to the school, Herman."

"It would be my pleasure," he said, nodding.

"Danke, mein Herr," I said.

"Can I go too, Sophie?" Willie asked.

"*Nein,* it's a girl's school. And you and I are going to continue lessons here in the hotel for now."

Willie cocked his head to one side. "And after that Papa will come and we'll all go home."

"*Ja,* Willie," I said, trying to sound sure but Willie is not easily fooled.

He sat pondering in the silence that followed.

"Then why is their papa here?"

Willie's question dropped like a cannon ball on the table. We all sat looking at it, wondering if it would explode.

I looked at Mama who had a high blush on her cheeks. She was thc first to speak.

"Willie, that is none of your business and rude of you to ask."

Tears came to Willie's eyes and he put his head in his hands. I wanted to take him in my arms but I could not move. We were guests in this hotel and Willie had insulted the owner.

Herr Menger broke the silence.

"Willie, it's not fair, I admit. But a certain Confederate general wanted our hotel to remain open for his officers to dine and wounded soldiers to be treated. And so I stayed."

Willie listened but did not show his face.

Herr Menger glanced at the nearest officers and lowered his voice.

"I always read your papa's political cartoons in our newspaper ... and agreed with him. He stood up for what he believed, while I straddle the fence." He paused. "Do you know what that means?"

Willie looked up and shook his head.

"It means I have one foot in the North and one in the South, depending on where I need to be."

"So you're on both sides?" Willie asked.

Herr Menger nodded thoughtfully. "You might say so."

"Then that means you don't fight because nobody fights himself."

"*Ja,* Willie, I don't fight and neither does your papa. He draws fighting and I run a hotel."

Smiling, Willie got out of his chair, ran to *Herr* Menger, and hugged him.

"So-o-o, looks like I have a third son — for the duration of the war anyway!"

With that, Peter and Babette threw themselves onto their father, claiming him. She crawled onto his lap while *Herr* Menger wrapped his arms around Peter and Willie. Louis, too old for such affectionate behavior, just looked at them with amusement."

"Come, Louis, and join the family."

Louis rose and stood behind his father, leaning over and putting his hands on his father's chest.

It was a lovely scene that warmed my heart and made me feel glad that we had come to San Antonio. But also made me want my papa back. The Confederate officers seemed to enjoy it as well, maybe thinking of their own families.

Now, as I sit writing tonight, I remember my first encounter with Confederate soldiers. It was a moonlit spring night early in the war before all the men had left. In Comfort we were having a dance party under the Schimmelpfennig Oak, where Chinese lanterns hung from the branches. To my surprise, Eduard asked me to dance. I stared at him for a moment, unable to speak, because he was my secret love. He took my hand, put his other hand at my waist, and we waltzed to the music. It was the first time he had ever touched me, and I wanted him never to let go.

And then everything stopped — the music, the dancing. Eduard released me, and I looked around. Some one hundred Confederate soldiers, all mounted on horses had approached our party. Their leader, Captain Duff, announced that Governor Lubbock had declared martial law and sent him to hang any man who refused to fight against the North. Soon after, Papa, Eduard, and other men left for Mexico.

Sunday
March 19, 1865

It was not long until *Frau* Menger asked me to help an injured Confederate soldier write a letter home. His room was down the hall from ours.

As we walked she said, "His right arm was amputated and now it has become infected. The doctor told him yesterday there is no cure for tetanus."

I gasped. "You mean he's going to die?"

"Probably."

When we came to his door, she knocked.

"Yes, come in," came a hoarse voice.

We entered.

Soft light from a shuttered window fell across the four-poster bed where the man lay. He turned his thin face toward us. His eyes were sad but I could tell that the nurse had taken good care of him because his dark hair was neatly combed and his beard and mustache trimmed. Still, none of that care could keep him alive.

What if he were Papa? He looked to be about the same age. I wondered if he had children.

Frau Menger spoke first. "Lieutenant Adams, may I introduce Miss Sophie Guenther who has kindly volunteered to write a letter for you."

"I am honored to meet you, Lieutenant," I said and made a slight curtsy.

A little smile curled the corners of his mouth. “I have a daughter about your age. Her name is Dorothy but we call her Dolly. She calls me Papa.”

“That’s what I call my father, too.”

I wondered if Dolly suspected that her father was dying from his wound.

“Is he fighting in the war?” the lieutenant asked.

I hesitated. I could not tell him that Papa was on the side of the Union.

“No, he has a bad leg and the army wouldn’t take him. Instead he got a job drawing battle scenes for a magazine.”

“Lucky man ... I was not so lucky.”

“I am sorry for that, sir.”

“And since I’ll never see my wife and family again, I need to write a final letter.”

That word, final, brought a lump to my throat.

“We need some fresh air,” *Frau* Menger said. She opened the shutters and pulled up the windows. A light breeze swept in, lifting the gauzy white curtains. “There, isn’t that better?”

“Much better,” I said.

Then she motioned me to a desk beside the bed. Hotel stationary, ink jar, and quill pen awaited.

I sat on the chair that had a velvet cushion and wiped my tears away. “Ready,” I told the lieutenant.

Frau Menger excused herself, and I waited, wondering if I could keep my composure.

“Before we begin I want to say something I cannot say to my wife.” He paused and tried to clear his raspy voice, to no avail.

“The North will soon win this war. My wife will have no slaves to work the cotton fields, and no husband to support her. I will have died in vain."

I turned to look into his sad blue eyes and felt myself wilt. What a useless war, I thought. People maimed and dying over slavery. It is madness! Suddenly it didn't matter which side he was on. A dying soldier is a dying soldier. It didn't even matter that he had slaves. It only mattered that his life was ruined — many people's lives were ruined forever.

"But there is no help for it," he said. "The damage is done. There is only this letter to write, so let's begin."

I nodded as I dipped the pen in the ink jar.

"To my beloved wife Nancy," he began and paused now and then as I wrote. "I bring you sad news, but you must stay strong for the children. I have developed a surgical disease, tetanus, for which there is no cure. Even now I have spasms that make breathing difficult, and sometimes my jaw is so tight that I can hardly speak. The doctor says I have only a few days to live."

He stopped for a time, seeming to gather his thoughts.

How does it feel to say that? I wondered. To know you will soon be no more? I could not bear it. I imagined his wife reading this awful news and sinking to the floor, holding the letter to her breast.

Then he went on. "Here is what I want you to do. Sell our place and take the children to live with your parents in Henderson. The South will lose this war, and the slaves will be freed. Therefore, sell the land."

It was good advice. Would she follow it? At least the family had somewhere to go.

The lieutenant sighed, sounding exhausted by the effort to speak and maybe by the sacrifice he made, perhaps for nothing if the North wins.

"Take your time, sir," I said in a wavery voice. "I am in no rush." In truth, I wanted to run out of the room and weep for him, weep for his wife and children and this senseless war.

Then he went on.

"I must end this letter now for I have no more strength or voice. A young girl named Sophie is writing my words. She reminds me of our Dolly.

"Know that I love you and the children and only wish I could embrace and kiss you once more.

"Your loving husband, David."

I lay down the pen and covered my eyes.

"You cry for me, Sophie?"

I dabbed my eyes, looked at him through the blur and nodded.

"Bless you, dear child."

"I don't want you to die, sir."

"There is no help for it, Sophie. Will you come when I do?"

My throat tightened. "Yes," I said in a strangled voice as I folded the letter and put it in the envelope. After writing his wife's address according to his dictation, I stood and said, "I promise," and walked from the room before I broke down weeping.

Please, *Gott,* don't let this happen to Papa or Eduard.

Thursday
March 23, 1865

This morning Willie and I sat on the couch in our parlor beside the open windows that overlook the courtyard. Mama had taken Lena there to play with Babette. The two girls, Babette in front and Lena behind, were riding a horse tricycle that the Mengers bought in France. Instead of a plain seat there was a horse with outstretched legs.

Meanwhile, Willie and I were having an arithmetic lesson.

"When we're done, can I go out and ride Babette's horse tricycle?" Willie asked.

"Of course, *Liebchen,* that will be your reward for working hard."

"Gut." He proceeded to count the beans that I spread on the low table before us.

"Twenty," he said.

"Take away three and what does that leave?"

He counted. "Seventeen."

"Now write the numbers on your slate and remember you have to borrow."

While he was writing, someone knocked on the door. I opened it and there stood *Frau* Menger with a big smile on her plump, rosy face and a letter in her hand.

"Gut news, Sophie!"

My heart leaped. "A letter for me?"

"*Nein,* but still *gut* news. It's a letter to me from Sister St. Marie, the Mother Superior, inviting you to come to Ursuline for an interview tomorrow. I thought you would want to know right away."

I caught my breath. "*Ja,* that is *gut* news. Thank you, *Frau* Menger."

After she left I sat down on the couch beside Willie and began to worry about questions the Mother Superior might ask. I wondered if she knew that people in Comfort are Freethinkers. Would she ask if I was one? And was I a Christian? What would I say to a Catholic nun? Would she refuse me if I were not a Christian, much less a Catholic?

Then Willie tapped my hand. "Sophie, what's the matter? She said it was *gut* news. Why are you frowning?"

"Because, dear Willie, I don't know what questions she will ask me and what I will answer."

Willie scooted closer and wrapped his arms around me. "Do you want to know what I think?"

"*Ja,* sure."

He leaned back. "Just tell the truth."

I looked into his bright blue eyes. He knew nothing of Catholics or the church or Freethinkers. But he was wise. Never underestimate a child's perception, especially Willie's.

"Some of her questions could be hard to answer," I went on.

"Like what?"

"Do you believe in *Gott?*"

"I don't even know what *Gott* is, Sophie."

"Neither do I."

He gave a decisive nod. "Then just say so."

For the rest of the morning I pondered Mother Superior's questions and my answers, even while Willie read aloud to me, and later while helping Mama and *Frau* Menger in the kitchen.

Friday
March 24, 1865

At ten o'clock this morning I met *Herr* Menger in the lobby.

"Guten Morgen, Sophie." Dressed in a black frock coat, trousers, white shirt and bow tie, he looked the successful man he was. I felt glad that I had worn my new blue and white sprigged calico and straw bonnet tied under my chin with blue ribbons.

"Our horses are saddled and await us out front." He motioned me toward the door.

There Mister Gravell, the hostler, held Pegasus and *Herr* Menger's shiny black horse. Pegasus dipped his head down and back up several times, nickering, when he saw me.

"Oh Peg, I'm glad to see you too." I stroked his silky white forehead.

Every day I go down to the stable and feed him some carrots from the kitchen. And every day Mister Gravell takes him out for a ride along the river.

"He's one of a kind, Miss Sophie," he said, giving me a hand up on the sidesaddle.

"Indeed," said *Herr* Menger, mounting his horse. "A pure white Arabian. How did you come by him?"

"My father bought him here in San Antonio on one of his trips. The Indians think he is Spirit Horse and stole him one night."

Herr Menger looked shocked. "But how did you get him back?"

"A Comanche chief, a friend of ours, brought him to me."

"Well, there are good Indians and bad Indians just like all other people," *Herr* Menger said.

Mister Gravell handed me the reins. "You can be sure he won't get stolen from my stable, Miss Sophie."

I nodded my thanks.

Across the street in Alamo Plaza, farmers' wagons, carriages, and horses surrounded the open city market, where women were buying fresh fruit and vegetables for the day.

"Time for us to be off, Sophie," *Herr* Menger said.

We left Alamo Plaza and turned right onto Commerce Street. It, too, was busy with oxcarts, wagons, carriages, and pedestrians of all races. We crossed a wooden bridge over the San Antonio River and rode on to a large open space that *Herr* Menger told me was called Main Plaza.

I gasped. Never in my life have I seen so many people doing so many different things, heading this way and that. I laughed when a boy on a horse galloped across the plaza in pursuit of a cow, trying to rope it, while two boys ran in the opposite direction, chasing their dog. Pegasus tossed his head and I stroked his neck.

"It's all right, Peg."

Across the plaza stood an old church with a bell tower on one side and a dome over the back part of the building.

"San Fernando Cathedral," *Herr* Menger said.

"Sometime I'd like to look inside," I told him.

"We can surely do that, Sophie. Mary would be delighted to take you there."

As we crossed the plaza, an older man tipped his hat in greeting and two ladies in a carriage nodded in recognition. *Herr* Menger returned the greetings by tipping his black derby.

"Everyone knows you, *mein Herr,"* I said.

"Ja, but it's not me. They like my beer, my hotel, and my wife's cooking." He laughed heartily, and I knew he was just being modest.

On the far side of the plaza we turned right on Acequia Street. It was lined with two-story shops of all kinds, a tailor, a bookstore, drugstore, saddle shop, a butcher, even a French restaurant. Anything one might want could be purchased here. I could not take it all in and wished I could stop for a moment and stare.

So many people greeted *Herr* Menger that he stopped lifting his hat and just touched the brim. They looked at me, probably wondering who I was, so I just smiled and nodded.

At last we came to a high stone wall on the right. Over the gate rose a wrought iron arch with the words "Ursuline Academy." My heart began to race. I had never seen a nun, much less spoken to one. Would she disapprove of me, a Freethinker, who had never read the Bible or been inside a church of any kind? *Ach,* there was so much I did not know about churches and the people who run them, especially Catholic nuns.

Herr Menger and I dismounted and entered. It was like stepping into another world, a quiet escape from the bustle of the city. I followed him along a path through a flower garden to a two-story building with galleries across both floors. There we tied our horses to hitching posts and stepped onto the gallery.

"You should address her as Reverend Mother, Sophie."

The door stood open on this sunny spring morning, and we stepped into a large entrance hall. The air was cooler than outside because of the thick white walls. Across the hall an open door gave a glimpse into a courtyard. A wooden cross hung above the door, the only decoration in the hall. Benches lined the walls. No girls were in sight although I could hear some voices, probably from classrooms.

Herr Menger led the way to a door on the right and knocked.

"Enter," came a woman's voice.

The small room we entered had only one window but the white walls reflected light from outside. The only color in the room came from a Mexican rug before the dark wooden desk. Behind the desk sat the Mother Superior. She rose and clasped her palms together as if praying for us.

"Welcome, *Herr* Menger and, I assume, Sophie."

Her flowing black habit with its wide white collar concealed her body. A black hood draped over a white cap hid her hair. All I could see was her face. Even though she was a woman of middle years, she had a youthful aura about her. Maybe it was her rounded cheeks or full lips or, most of all, her lively eyes.

On the wall behind her hung a wooden cross with the limp form of Jesus nailed to it. I shuddered to think of the pain. Back then they crucified people. Today they hang them. *Will we ever learn not to kill each other?*

I bowed with my palms together, following her example. "Yes, Reverend Mother, I am Sophie Guenther."

"I leave her in your care, Reverend Mother," *Herr* Menger said then, "while I wander in your garden if I may."

"Of course," she replied.

After he stepped out, she turned to me. "Please, sit down, Sophie." She gestured to a straight wooden chair in front of her desk, and we both sat. It had armrests and a carved backrest, but there was nothing restful about the chair. It demanded alertness.

She studied me for a moment in silence. I felt a little quiver in my body as I waited for her to speak. It was as if my life depended on being accepted here. I clasped my hands in my lap to keep from squirming and wondered what her first question would be. *The truth, Sophie. Tell her the truth like Willie said.*

"I have heard much about you from Emma Altgelt, about your love of reading and journaling and your help in her school," she began.

It wasn't a question after all — it was praise. I smiled and relaxed just a bit.

"Yes, Reverend Mother, she took over from our teacher when he had to go fight in the war." I paused but she seemed to be waiting for more. So I went on. "She assigned reading to my friend and me — works by Homer and Shakespeare and Goethe, which we then discussed, as well as some history and geography. But I'm sure there are gaps in my education which would be filled in here."

She nodded. "Yes, like philosophy, astronomy, botany, languages, especially French, and my favorite, ancient history, which I teach. Did you know that Cleopatra spoke nine languages and rarely needed an interpreter?"

"No, I didn't but that makes me want to learn more about ancient Egypt."

"Well, if I grant you admission, you will study that and more."

A thrill prickled my skin. "Everything my father dreamed of for my education."

"Yes, I know of your father from his editorial cartoons. Where is he now?"

"I wish I knew. He was wounded in the Nueces River Massacre while trying to escape to Mexico and join the Union Army. Later, even though his leg was never the same, he managed to sail to New York, where he got a job drawing battle scenes for *Harper's Weekly*."

"So being wounded saved him from having to fight in this terrible war."

I nodded. "But I still fear for his life."

"You must pray for him."

Again I nodded. Even though I do not understand who or what I'm praying to, I pray when I'm afraid.

"Speaking of prayer," she began.

A pang of fear shot through my heart. *Here it comes,* I thought. *The Freethinker question. Could my answer keep me from being accepted? If I tell the truth will she reject me as a student?*

"I believe you come from a community of so-called Freethinkers. Since I am not sure exactly what that means, could you explain?"

I took a deep breath. "Reverend Mother, it means that we read many books and want to be free to think for ourselves instead of accepting traditional beliefs without question."

"Do you read the Bible as well?"

I hesitated. Could the truth ruin my chances of acceptance? Once again I remembered Willie's words.

"We never owned a Bible."

The words hung in the air for a moment.

"If you read many books, why is the Bible not one of them?"

Strangely, that was a question that occurred to me before.

"I've wondered that myself, Reverend Mother, especially after learning about the Twenty-third Psalm."

She smiled. "And how did that happen?"

"I learned about it when I rode out to the Nueces River to find my father after we heard he was wounded."

Mother Superior leaned forward in her chair and looked at me with concern in her eyes. "Alone? You rode out there alone?"

"Yes, without my mother's permission. But with the help of a friendly Indian, I found my father and brought him home."

She leaned back and put her hand over her heart. "You are a very brave girl, Sophie. I cannot imagine doing such a thing."

"I was scared but I could not bear to think of his dying alone in the wilderness ... and that gave me courage."

She nodded. "So now tell me about the Bible reading."

I began to feel a little more at ease with her.

"On the way to the Nueces I spent a night at a Christian lady's cabin. Her husband and sons had all gone to the war so she lived alone out in that wilderness. She asked me to read the Psalm aloud from her Bible to give us both the courage to face whatever comes."

Mother Superior picked up a Bible from her desk and opened it. After leafing through the pages, she said, "Let's hear it again." She gave the book to me and I read aloud.

"The Lord is my shepherd; I shall not want.
He maketh me to lie down in green pastures;

he leadeth me beside the still waters. He restoreth my soul; he leadeth me in the paths of righteousness for his name's sake. Yea, though I walk through the valley of the shadow of death, I will fear no evil, for thou art with me; thy rod and thy staff they comfort me."

"And did the Psalm help?"

"Yes, I even copied it into my journal and remembered the words, when it seemed to me that I was actually walking through the valley of the shadow of death to find my father."

She looked at me for a moment, her lips pursed.

"From what I understand, Freethinkers do not believe in God. Did your experience make a believer of you?"

"Reverend Mother, I think Freethinkers just want to be free to believe what they will. I don't know what God is but I like what my father said."

"And what was that?"

"He said there is a great mystery of the universe and we can only catch a glimpse of what that means."

"One may find God in the mystery," Mother Superior said. "And that is where faith comes in."

Blind faith, Papa would say. I looked down so she could not see my thoughts.

"I appreciate your honesty and openness, Sophie, and that you are searching for answers to the mystery, as your father calls it."

She sat forward, elbows on the desk, and clasped her hands together, resting her chin on them. "So now, tell me what is it you wish to do with your education?"

I had not expected this question and had only a dream for an answer. Still, I felt she liked me and might understand.

"I have long had a dream of becoming a writer. That's one reason I keep a journal."

"And how will you earn a living until such time as you may attain success?"

I shook my head. She appreciated honesty and so I gave an honest answer. "I don't know. I had not thought that far ahead."

"Well, there are ways for an educated young lady to earn a living, such as teaching or becoming a governess in a wealthy household. *Frau* Altgelt wrote to me about your teaching abilities."

I thought of *Tante*'s home school and remembered how much I enjoyed teaching the little ones to read. It was like opening a door to the world for them.

"That sounds like something I would love."

She nodded. "Good, and one more question. What do you dream of writing?"

"A novel, I think."

"About what?"

For some reason — though I had not thought of it before — I said, "Cleopatra."

Mother Superior chuckled. "Yes, I think she has been much maligned by Roman propaganda and male historians, as I teach in my ancient history course."

She paused, studying me with her kind eyes, and I met her gaze. I liked this lady and wanted to attend her school, wanted to learn ancient history from her. If only my God questions did not disqualify me in her judgment.

Finally she spoke.

"As I said, I like your honesty and open mind, Sophie. You are a bright young lady, but you still have much to learn."

I caught and held my breath until she continued.

"And I invite you to learn it here."

I thrilled at her invitation. Papa's and my dream come true.

"If you wish to do so," she continued, "you must agree to attend worship services in the chapel along with all the other girls. That is a requirement. Attendance is all I ask, not acceptance of Catholic beliefs. Of course I will expect you to keep any criticism to yourself so as not to influence other girls. And I will hope for your eventual conversion."

I did not mind attending chapel services. I could learn about Christianity and think about it however I wished.

"Reverend Mother, I am honored to accept and gladly agree to your requirements." I paused, wondering whether I would live at the school or the Menger. "Will I be living here?"

"Yes, Sophie. I am pleased to tell you that Emma Altgelt has offered to pay your tuition and board for one year."

My hand flew to my heart. "Bless her!"

"Yes, *Frau* Altgelt thinks highly of you and believes you deserve a good education." She stood. "And I think you will make a fine addition to our community."

"Thank you, Reverend Mother. I will do my best."

"Until then ... farewell, Sophie."

I wanted to hug her but dared not. I stepped out into the entrance hall, which was filled with girls of all ages, little girls and girls like me, wearing all manner of dresses, some fancy, some plain. They chattered happily among themselves and several cast glances at me. I smiled as I made my way to the door, knowing I would be one of them in September. Papa would be so happy to know.

Now, back at the Menger, I must stop writing in this journal and write Papa a letter. I hope he will receive it, but in time of war nothing is certain.

Sunday
March 26, 1865

Two days ago I wrote that nothing is certain in war. But that is not true. Death is certain. It happens everywhere to thousands of soldiers, and this afternoon it happened to Lieutenant Adams.

Exactly one week after I wrote the lieutenant's letter for him, there was a gentle knock on our door. Mama, Willie and Lena were napping while I read the first volume of Gibbon's history of Rome that *Tante* loaned me.

I opened the door and there stood a matronly woman in a dark dress and immaculate white apron. "I'm Alma Akin, nurse for Lieutenant Adams. Are you Sophie?"

I felt something drop inside me. "Yes, is he dying?"

She nodded solemnly. "And he's asking for you."

I did not want to see him or anyone die. But how could I refuse? His family was not here, and I reminded him of his daughter. I was his only family. If he were Papa, far from home and yearning for us, what would I want someone to do?

I followed Nurse Akin to his room, where the door stood open.

"He told me not to close it because he didn't want to die alone," she whispered.

No one should die alone, I thought.

Lieutenant Adams lay with his eyes half closed, mouth

open, his chest heaving for breath.

The shutters were closed so I opened them and pulled up the windows. I could not bear for him to die in an airless room, cut off from the world.

He struggled to fully open his eyes but could not. Then he raised his left arm, searching for me. I took his hand in mine.

"Dolly?" he said in a tight voice, barely opening his mouth.

I caught my breath. He thought I was his daughter. What should I do? I looked at Nurse Akin, standing on the other side of his bed, and she nodded.

"Yes, Papa." My voice wavered with the strange reality of this drama.

"Good ..." He tried to clear his throat.

Was it cruel to pretend I was his daughter? I wondered.

"I'm dying," he whispered, clutching my hand as if holding onto me would keep him alive.

At that moment, I became Dolly and he became my father.

"No, Papa, no, don't leave me," I wailed as tears ran down my cheeks. I clasped his hand in both of mine and stared at the side of his face.

He turned to me then. "Oh, dear child ..." he gasped. "Read ... the Bible."

On the bedside table lay a black leather Bible. I turned to the Twenty-third Psalm, and read the last four lines.

> "Yea, though I walk through the valley of
> the shadow of death, I will fear no evil,
> for thou art with me; thy rod and thy
> staff they comfort me."

"Fear no evil," he repeated. He sighed and seemed to sink into the bed, his grip on my hand loosening.

I stared at him, watching the artery in his neck throb for another few minutes and then stop.

I lay my head on his shoulder and wept. He was gone, dead. I have watched two men die. Who is next? People say that a soldier's death is a good death. But there is no such thing.

After a time I looked up at Nurse Akin.

She said, "I've seen many deaths, some fighting it, some accepting it. At least this poor man believed he died in his daughter's arms."

I nodded but could not speak.

Wednesday
April 12, 1865

The good news came over the telegraph wires — the war has ended! Finally I got what I wanted for my birthday. On April 9th General Robert E. Lee surrendered to General Ulysses S. Grant, our "Odysseus," at the Appomattox Court House in Virginia. The war began on my twelfth birthday in 1861 and ended just before my sixteenth birthday, which is today. Four long years and hundreds of thousands dead. What madness!

Hopefully, Papa and Eduard will soon be coming home but we have not heard from either one since early this year. And as I said before, nothing is certain in war but death. A frightening thought that hung over me this day.

This morning I stepped out to the hotel gallery that faces Alamo Square, curious to know what people thought about the news. The market was busy but quieter than usual, almost solemn. It seemed that everyone, including me, is just relieved that the hopeless war is over, no matter who won. Many have lost loved ones or are wondering when they will be home, just as I am.

In the evening *Frau* Menger gave a party for me. She and Mama baked my favorite chocolate cake. Even when so many food items are not available because of the blockade, her husband managed to get all kinds of delicacies

— like chocolate — from Mexico.

As we gathered at their big oval table, *Herr* Menger stood and proposed a toast. "Here's to our young friend Sophie on her sixteenth birthday ..." He lowered his voice because there were some Confederate officers in the dining room. "... and the end of the war."

"Yay!" Willie exclaimed as he stood and pumped his arms.

The younger Menger children, Peter and Babette, followed Willie's example. Four Confederate officers sitting nearby looked around at us.

Herr Menger spoke to them. "We only celebrate this young lady's sixteenth birthday. My apologies."

He was not only a good businessman, he was a diplomat. Maybe that is the same thing.

The officers nodded and turned back to their own table, all except Willie's friend, the saluting one. He looked directly at Willie.

"Didn't I tell you I would pass on your words to General Lee, young man?"

For a moment Willie stared at him in wonder.

"You really did?" he squeaked.

"Well, somehow he got the idea and put an end to the fighting – just like you said."

The officer gave him another salute and Willie returned it.

"Did I really end the war, Sophie?"

We all laughed and Willie wilted.

"Nein, Willie, but you made a friend of the enemy, and that helped end the war."

After *Frau* Menger sliced the cake and passed plates around, *Herr* Menger took the rest to the four officers. With smiles on their faces they turned and lifted their wine glasses to me.

"Happy Birthday, Miss."

If only the war could have been settled so easily. If only Odysseus had offered the suitors chocolate cake instead of slaughtering them. It seems to me that there are other ways of settling differences than slaughter.

Saturday
April 15, 1865

Then came the bad news, unbelievable news.

We were having breakfast at our table in the Colonial Room when *Herr* Menger strode in, looking distraught.

"I've just come from the telegraph office," he announced to all. He paused and braced himself. "President Lincoln was shot last night while attending a play ... and died this morning." He shook his head. "His doctors could not save him."

There was utter silence in the room. For a moment no one moved or spoke. We were all stunned — even the Confederate officers did not seem to know how to react. The war was over and the president dead. No matter which side you were on, both lost.

Willie broke the silence in his high-pitched voice.

"Why is everyone killing each other, Sophie?"

"I don't know, Willie."

Lena came to Mama and crawled into her lap. "Is somebody going to kill us?"

Mama hugged her close. *"Nein, Liebchen.* I'll keep you safe."

Then she turned to me and said quietly, "I want to leave this uncivilized country. It's no place to raise my babies."

"You always say that, Mama, but you know Papa can never go back. We have to wait until he comes home and builds our new house, and then all will be well."

"We don't know whether he is coming home or not, Sophie."

"He *is* coming home, Mama," Willie said, "and I'm not a baby."

But Mama was right — I didn't know and neither did Willie. We were just hoping and waiting.

Meanwhile, poor Mrs. Lincoln. I remember when her son Willie died of typhoid fever. She was in deep mourning. And now her husband. Can she bear it? Can any of us bear what war brings?

Wednesday April 27, 1865

We waited, we hoped, and then the unthinkable happened. As I write, Willie is sitting on the floor under the desk, hugging my legs and occasionally whimpering. Now and then I lay down my pen and stroke his curly blond hair as if he were a puppy and say, "Willie, Willie." Tears run down my cheeks, and I wipe them away angrily because I am helpless.

Here is how the devastating news arrived. As our family started up the stairs to our room after dinner this afternoon, *Herr* Menger called to us from the front desk in the lobby.

"*Frau* Guenther, I have mail for you, a letter and ... a haversack." He paused. "I hope it's not ... I hope it's good news."

Alarm sprang up inside me. A haversack? Papa's? I rushed to him, hoping the letter was from Papa. But the handwriting was not his, which set my heart pounding. I handed the letter to Mama and put the strap of the haversack over my shoulder, the ominous haversack.

Upstairs in our parlor, Mama opened the letter slowly as if she was afraid of what was inside — for good reason. After she read to herself, she sank down on the upholstered armchair and dropped the letter on the floor.

"What, Mama, what is it?" I said.

"Ach, Kinder, your papa is not coming home — ever." And then she put her face in her hands. "How could he do this to me? Such a foolish man."

For a moment I could not breathe or move or speak. I wanted everything to stop and go back, back before those awful words. Back, back, back ...

Willie and Lena ran to Mama. Lena crawled onto her lap and began sucking her thumb, which she had not done in a long time. She was only a few months old when Papa left and probably has no memory of him, but she surely feels grief through us. Willie just clung to Mama's knees. I stood, staring at them in disbelief that this was happening.

Then Mama's words, *such a foolish man,* sent a jolt of anger through my body.

"Nein! Papa was *not* foolish," I screamed. "How dare you say that? Didn't you love him? Didn't you?" I panted for breath, wild eyed with anger.

Mama looked at me, frowning. *"Ja,* Sophie, more than he loved me or he never would have left us."

"You know he had no choice, Mama," I said in a shrill voice.

"No fighting!" Willie cried as he ran to me and wrapped his arms around my waist.

I looked down at him and put my hand on his head. After taking some deep breaths, I asked him to hand me the letter. He did so and I flung the haversack on the couch and collapsed beside it. Willie crawled up and put his head on my arm.

I read this letter through the blur of tears:

New York, N.Y.
April 4, 1865

Dear Madam,

It is with great sorrow that I must inform you of the death of your husband, Friedrich Guenther. He was mortally wounded at the Battle of Petersburg on March 25th in Virginia by the explosion of a cannonball nearby.

Harper's arranged for his burial in the Green Wood Cemetery in Brooklyn and ordered a headstone.

He was an extraordinary artist, one of our best, and we shall miss him, as I am sure you and your family will.

Along with this letter I am sending a haversack of his belongings, which he asked me to return to you in case of his death. May these items be of comfort in your grief.

Respectfully,
George Curtis
Editor
Harper's Weekly

My papa buried? In Brooklyn? Never to return? I shook my head. *Nein, bitte Gott,* don't let it be true.

I lay the letter aside and picked up the haversack. Slowly I unbuckled the flap and looked inside. There was another letter, a drawing tablet, pencils, watercolor kit, quill, a bottle of ink, and a tin plate and cup. Willie leaned closer to peek in.

I pulled out the letter. "This is from Papa. Shall I open it, Mama?"

"*Ja,* and read aloud."

Here is what he wrote, and Mama let me paste it in my journal:

January 29, 1865
New York, N.Y.

Liebe Elisabet, Sophie, Willie, and Lena,

It is with halting hand that I take up my pen to write this final letter, which you will receive should I not return.

The thought of never seeing you again, digs deep into my heart. Never to hold you in my arms and kiss you, is more than I can bear. But I must, for nothing is certain in war.

How I have longed for this war to end so that I could come home and embrace you. But now that is not to be. Please try to understand my insistence on joining the war. I know you wanted to keep me safe, but, as I once told Sophie, there are things worse than death. And that is not being true to oneself. I have been true to myself.

Liebe Elisabet I am sending a money order for you to book passage back to Germany as you have always wanted. I hope you will forgive me for bringing you to Texas. Now you must sell the land to Arlis or give it to him as needed.

And to you, Sophie, my darling daughter, promise me that you will pursue your dream of being a writer. We spoke of Ursuline Academy but there are also many good schools in Germany. Lastly, if Eduard should survive this awful war, you will have a difficult decision to make. Be my strong girl, and most of all be true to yourself.

Now for Willie. If only I could see the man you

will become and know your dreams. Mine are finished but yours have just begun. Your future awaits in Dresden. Make the most of it and take care of your mother and sisters.

And Lena, my beloved baby girl. As you grow up, I only hope you can remember how much I loved you. May your life as a young lady in Dresden be filled with happiness and success at whatever endeavors you may choose.

Do not mourn me for I will always be with you. Always. How is that possible? you may ask. I do not know but I believe that love is deathless. It lasts forever. Think of me, say my name, and I will come to you in a dream or on a gentle breeze.

Your loving husband and father,
Friedrich (Papa)

"I promise, Papa." I lay the letter on my lap and wept.

Willie and I sat on the couch huddled together for a long time, one or the other of us weeping. I felt empty. The worst thing I could imagine had happened.

What now? I wondered. All I knew for sure was that I had to be strong and true to myself.

Then Willie whispered, "Papa?"

After a time, he stirred and turned to me. "I felt Papa's arms around me."

"Oh Willie." I cupped his sweet, tearful face in my hands. "That makes my heart glad. Now let's see what else is in the haversack."

I took out the tablet, opened it, and found Papa's self portrait.

"It's Papa!" Willie shouted. "Mama, come look, it's

Papa, only with a beard!"

But she did not move. Her eyes were closed and her cheeks wet with tears as she held Lena in her lap.

I looked back at the portrait. Papa's dark eyes gazed sadly at me, as if saying he was sorry not to come home. Had it really been three years since I last saw him? Except for the beard he looked the same but he wasn't. Now everything had changed.

Papa is never coming back — never! He is gone forever. *Ach,* how can I bear it? How can I be as strong as Odysseus? I'm just a sixteen-year-old girl who does not know how to survive this awful loss.

I want him back ... I want him back to speak Latin to me, to watch him draw and paint, to show me how to be true to myself, to hold me in his arms when I am sad. But there is no help for it.

After a time Mama came and sat on my other side with Lena on her lap. I handed her Papa's drawing.

She shook her head. *"Ach,* my handsome Friedrich. I cannot believe you are gone for good."

"Where do you go when you die?" Willie asked.

"No one knows, *Liebchen,"* Mama said.

"Then I don't want to die and I don't want you or Sophie or Lena to die — ever."

"Me either," Lena said.

"Willie, Lena, I'll tell you what Papa told me when I said the same thing to him."

"What?" they asked in unison.

"He said everything grows and changes. You will grow up and marry and have children of your own, who will grow and change."

"And then I'll die?" Willie asked.

"Ja, a long, long time from now. Too long to even think about. But now we are alive and must make the best of it." I was telling myself as well as Willie.

After a long silence, Mama took a deep breath and sat up. "Well, speaking of change, there is nothing to keep us here any longer. So now we go home to Germany as soon as the blockade opens. Your grandparents will be so happy."

But what about Eduard? I thought. *She seemed to be ignoring what Papa said about him.*

Maybe Willie sensed what was going on in my mind because he suddenly sat up and looked me in the eye.

"What did Papa mean when he said you will have a difficult decision to make?"

I did not know how to answer. Willie would be devastated if I stayed here. In my silence, Willie answered for me.

"I know what he meant ... that you have to decide between us and Eduard. Is that right, Sophie?"

I bit my lips together.

"Say it, Sophie!"

I could not so I nodded.

"Nein," Willie yelled, throwing himself on top of me and wrapping his arms around my neck.

Mama turned to me. "Sophie, no matter what your papa wrote, there is no question. You are coming with the family. I cannot lose both a husband and a daughter."

I said no more, but if Eduard comes home, what will I do?

Sunday
May 29, 1865

I have lost Papa. It has been a month since the awful news arrived, and I still think of him every day and want him back. It is so lonely without him. Even though he was far away, he was in this world. His letters were proof. Now I don't know where he is. But someday . . . someday, I will travel to New York and place flowers on Papa's grave and call his name.

And Eduard. Have I also lost him? The last letter I received was in January, and it was written in December. Since then, nothing. The war is over so why has he not come home? Six weeks have passed, plenty of time for him to return to Comfort, and people there know where I am. So I fear the worst ... but cling to hope. Still it is hard to keep hoping he is alive after losing Papa. It seems like everyone and everything I love is taken from me — Papa, our house on the hill, Papa's paintings, our border collie Max, and now Pegasus, since we are leaving Texas.

Maybe Mama is right about going back to Germany — I don't know. I don't know anything anymore. She is trying to book passage for us but so far the agent here in San Antonio has not been able to do so. It seems that ships are only carrying soldiers and equipment.

I can only thank *Gott* for the Mengers. They have been so kind and thoughtful since the news came about Papa.

Herr Menger took Willie for a ride around San Antonio on his horse, stopped at a store, and bought him a stuffed bear made in Germany. Willie named him Papa Bear and sleeps with him every night. *Frau* Menger bought a baby doll for Lena with a pink bonnet on her head and eyes that open and close. Lena named her Baby Girl.

Every day I ride Pegasus along the San Antonio River with Mister Gravell riding one of the other horses in his care. Peg has no idea that Mama is taking our family back to Germany. When I asked her if we could take him, she said *nein*.

This afternoon Mama and I were sitting in our parlor while the little ones napped. Mama was at the desk writing a letter to her parents, and I was rereading Eduard's last letter in my journal.

My thoughts were suddenly interrupted.

"Sophie," Mama said.

I looked up.

She had laid down her pen and turned to me.

"You are going to love our new life, living in my parents' big house, going to plays, the opera, art galleries. And we will find a school for you."

"But no Papa," I said. "Do you not miss him?"

"Of course I do." She smoothed back a strand of blond hair that came loose from the coiled braid circling her head.

I could not tell if she really did or was just saying so.

"When I look at you I am reminded of him," she went on. "Your brown eyes, your curly dark hair, your dimples when you smile. I only wish you would smile more."

"There is not much to smile about right now. Everything has changed."

"And it is about to change for the better as soon as I can manage to book our passage back to Germany. After all, Sophie, that's what your papa wanted."

"But I'm not sure it is what I want."

"What do you want then?"

"I want to wait for Eduard."

"I'm not leaving you here, Sophie. You will have a much better life in Germany."

"Can't we just wait and see if he comes back?"

"If he hasn't come by now, he's not coming."

"You can't know that for sure, Mama."

"Even if he does, I'm not leaving you here. You are too young to know what is best for you."

"That is not what Papa thinks. He said I would have a difficult decision to make."

"The decision is mine, your mother, Sophie."

"How old were you when you decided to marry Papa and go to Texas, against your parents' will?"

She drew in a long breath. "Eighteen, but two years makes a big difference."

"Mama, it is true that I don't wish to stay here if Eduard doesn't return. But for now, can't we just agree on that? Should he by some miracle come back, then the difficult decision can be made. But if we leave and find out later that he returned, that he was alive and I never got to see him to even say farewell, it would break my heart."

"Whatever happens, Sophie, it will be my decision."

Just then Willie and Lena wandered into the parlor looking sleepy eyed, and our discussion was over.

This evening *Frau* Menger invited us to have dinner at their family table, which cheered me. We dined on stewed lamb with dumplings, a delicious specialty of hers. Mama made apple pie for dessert.

"So, Elizabet," *Herr* Menger began, "I know you are eager to return to Germany. Have you managed to book passage to Galveston now that the blockade has been lifted?"

"Not yet, William. The booking agent here informed me that civilians are currently barred from travel out of Indianola. Only soldiers are allowed."

He wiped his mouth with a napkin and nodded. "I've heard so. However, I happen to have a friend who is captain of the steamship *Clinton.* Captain Talbot by name, an obliging gentleman. I think he would make an exception for your family. So just leave it to me."

Mama thanked him.

"Not that I am eager for you to depart but I know you are."

"Yes, I have written my family to tell them we're coming home."

"It's a shame, though, that Sophie won't be attending Ursuline Academy," *Frau* Menger said. "I thought it was the perfect place for her."

"It's what Papa wanted for me," I said.

"His last wishes were for us to go back to Dresden, Sophie," Mama reminded me.

"I know ..." I could not bring myself to talk about Papa's saying I would have to make a difficult decision, not here with the whole Menger family watching and listening. It was a private family matter.

Sitting beside me at the round table, Willie lay his fork down on his plate and turned to me, his eyes alarmed. "Sophie, you're coming to Germany with us, aren't you?"

I hesitated,

"Aren't you?" he demanded.

"I think so."

"What do you mean you *think* so?"

Everyone at the table stopped eating and looked at me.

"Of course she is, Willie," Mama said.

Willie was not convinced and I could not lie to him. Thankfully he said no more.

I looked around at the Menger family and smiled, as if to say, it's all right.

No one spoke or ate a bite until *Herr* Menger broke the silence.

"I know this must be a hard decision, just as hard as when we left Germany to come here. But one does what must be done."

I nodded in agreement. *Whatever that may be,* I thought.

"You are fortunate to have family there," he went on, "but I happen to love the freedom here in this new country, the freedom to be what you want to be."

"I'm going to be a fireman," said eight-year-old Peter in his serious manner.

"Me too," Babette said.

Peter laughed and said, "You can't be a fireman."

"Papa said I can be whatever I want to be."

"But you're not a man so how can you be a fire*man*?"

Babette turned to her papa.

"Well, my dear," he said, "as captain of the volunteer fire department, I think you could be the first fire*woman* in the world if you want!"

Everyone laughed.

"Dear child," *Frau* Menger began, "if I can own and

run a hotel, you can be a firewoman."

Babette grinned and then stuck out her tongue at Peter.

"And I," elder brother Louis said, "will help Mama and Papa run this hotel someday."

"What about you, Willie?" asked *Herr* Menger.

Willie squirmed in his chair for a moment.

"I think I will go to art school in Dresden and be an artist like Papa." He looked around at everyone for approval.

I patted him on the back. "Oh, Willie, that is perfect."

"Now for Lena," *Herr* Menger said. "What will you be, *Fräulein?*"

Lena looked at Mama for a moment.

Then she said, "A piano player like Mama."

Mama smiled at her. "Then you will have lessons in Dresden."

"And how about you, Sophie?" *Frau* Menger asked.

"I have always wanted to be a writer, which is why I keep a journal."

"Well, I am pleased that your futures are all planned," *Herr* Menger said. "Now, my dear, what's for dessert?"

"Elisabet's apple pie," *Frau* Menger told him.

After dinner Mama sat down at the piano in the lobby. Willie and Lena stood on either side to watch her play, while I stood behind her. She turned to each of them in turn, saying, "This piece by Robert Schumann was a favorite of your papa's. It's called *Träumerie* or Dreaming. Listen and see if you can imagine what the dream is about."

As she began the slow, soft piece, her fingers taking their time, lingering over the keys, tears came to my eyes. I remembered standing at the bottom of the stairs one night in our old house and watching her play this piece, while Papa stood behind her, his hands on her shoulders, her golden hair undone from its braid. Earlier they had argued about his decision to join the Union Army, and this was their way of making up.

Was she remembering too?

When she finished playing, she turned to Willie. "What do you think, *Liebchen?*"

"I think the dream is about Papa being here with us." As Willie looked up at her, I could see tears on his cheeks and on Mama's too. Maybe she really did love Papa and is determined to keep us safe.

After supper, Mama sat on the couch with Willie and Lena snuggled close to read from a book of fairy tales that *Frau* Menger loaned us.

"Which one tonight?" she asked.

"The Frog Prince," Willie said, hugging Papa Bear close.

I sat down at the desk, lighted the brass Sophie and Eduard oil lamps, and started writing a letter to Eduard. Instead I got caught up in the story about the frog who turns into a prince when the princess kisses him.

When Mama finished reading, Willie asked, "Is that a true story?"

"Nein, it's a fairy tale," she said.

I lay down my pen. "But there is truth in fairy tales, Willie. And the truth is that a kiss, which means love, can make magic happen."

"So if I kiss Papa Bear, he could turn into Papa?"

"In your imagination."

"But not really?"

"You can pretend."

Willie kissed Papa Bear and smiled.

It was not enough but it was something.

"Now, time to get ready for bed, *Liebchen,"* Mama said.

"I'll be in to say goodnight," I told Willie and Lena, and took up my pen.

I had no idea where Eduard was, so I simply addressed it to him in care of the Army of Tennessee. Maybe he has to walk all the way home and will soon arrive. If only I could know.

I wrote him about Papa and how we were living in San Antonio and that we were going back to Germany. I said I have no choice in the matter because Mama will not hear of my staying in Texas. And since I have not heard from you in such a long time, I wonder if you will ever return.

Sunday
June 18, 1865

Still no word from Eduard. Where is he? I fear I will never see him again. Either he is no longer in this world or I will no longer be in Texas. I had a letter from Etta, saying that his mother has not heard from him and fears the worst. But I refuse to give up hope.

As for leaving Texas, *Herr* Menger told us that Captain Talbot will allow our family to board his ship, the *Clinton*. He has a few officer quarters and will reserve one for us. It seems that *Herr* Menger can make most anything happen. He has a convincing way with people, and everyone likes him.

Captain Talbot sails from Indianola on July 19th, so we have to leave San Antonio on July 12th, only three weeks from now. It is all planned. *Ach*, I hardly know what to think. I cling to the idea that Eduard is alive somewhere. But I am afraid to insist on staying here without knowing. I would be alone in the world. And Willie would be devastated if I did not go with the family.

He has taken to drawing in Papa's tablet, using his graphite pencils, the very art materials that Papa used on the battlefield.

"Do you think Papa would mind?" Willie asked me before he started.

"Nein," I said. "He would love the idea of his son carrying on his talent."

Willie grinned and proceeded to draw everything in sight or in his head, Babette's horse tricycle, Pegasus, *Herr* Menger, Papa Bear, even himself.

This morning after breakfast he said, "Sophie, can I draw you?"

"Of course, Willie. Let's go out to the courtyard."

Mama smiled as she helped Lena buckle her shoes. "Good idea, Willie."

"Me too," Lena said.

"Nein, Liebchen, you and I are going for a stroll in the plaza like ladies. Here is your little pink bonnet." Mama slipped it over Lena's dark, curly hair and tied the ribbons. Then she put on her own straw bonnet.

The day was sunny and warm, so Willie and I sat on a bench under one of the cottonwood trees just outside the dining room windows, Willie on one end, straddling the bench, and I on the other, sitting ladylike and turning my face to him.

He opened the haversack, laid Papa's tablet on the bench before him, and brought out a graphite pencil. Then he studied me for a moment, just as I had seen Papa do. I had on my blue sprigged calico dress with a lace collar. My hair was clasped with a silver barrette on each side, letting my curls hang down to my shoulders.

I watched as Willie drew an oval for my head, dark scribbles for my hair, a smiling mouth, and dots for dimples. He seemed totally absorbed, looking up at me, then down at his drawing.

When he was done, he held the tablet up for me to see. "It's not as good as Papa's drawing," he said.

"Oh, Willie, I love it and I bet it's as good as Papa could draw when he was six years old."

"Do you think I can be an artist like him?"

"I think so, if you keep on looking and drawing. Papa always said that when he was a boy, he had a passion to draw everything he saw. If you do the same, you can be an artist like him. And that is a beautiful way to keep him alive."

Willie's delicate little mouth curled up in a smile. "I like that, Sophie. And when we go back to Germany, I can have art lessons."

I nodded. *"Ja,* and go to a real school."

"You're coming too, aren't you, Sophie?"

"Ja," I said without enthusiasm.

Willie frowned. "But you don't want to?"

"I don't have a choice, Willie, and it would make me very sad not to go with you."

"Me too." He slid off the bench and wrapped his arms around my neck.

"But it also makes me sad to leave all our friends behind."

"Like Etta?"

"Ja, and *Tante* and ..."

"Eduard?"

"How did you know?"

"Well, I know you write letters to each other."

"Ja, but I haven't received one in a long time."

Willie frowned. "Do you think he was killed, like Papa?"

"I don't know, Willie."

"What if he comes back? Will you stay here?"

How could this little boy know my mind?

"Who would you rather stay with?" he went on. "Eduard or us?"

"Ach, don't ask me such a question, Willie."

"Choose us, Sophie."

I hugged him, wondering how I could ever part with him. Better not to think about it since Eduard was probably not coming home, which brought an ache to my throat.

After a time I released him. "Now I need to go upstairs and write some letters to friends in Comfort about our leaving."

Willie climbed back on the bench. "And I'm going to stay here and draw this tree."

"Papa would be pleased," I said. "Just come upstairs and show it to me when you finish."

He nodded, turned to a blank page in the tablet, picked up the pencil, and studied the tree.

Back in our parlor alone, I sat down at the desk and wrote a letter to *Tante*. I thanked her for her offer to pay my tuition and board at Ursuline, but told her that we had passage back to Germany next month.

It was hard to write Etta, especially since I had promised to come back to Comfort. But promises get broken during times of war. I imagined her reading the letter, leaping in a stagecoach, coming here, and whisking me back to Comfort.

Ach, I will never have a friend like her again. And I will never have a true love like Eduard either.

Tuesday
July 11, 1865

This evening before supper we were doing our last minute packing when someone knocked on our door. I opened it to *Herr* Menger.

"There is a young man in the lobby asking for you, Sophie."

My heart jumped and I gasped. Could it be? I stared at *Herr* Menger for a moment, my mouth open.

"Eduard Meyer by name," he continued. "Quite a fine young man, I must say. We've had a little talk."

I thought I might fall down. *Herr* Menger took his leave, and Willie ran to me and wrapped his arms around my waist.

"Sophie, don't ..." He did not finish, just held on to me.

I let him hold me for a moment and then unwrapped his arms and cupped his face in my hands. "Willie, I'll be back."

Mama came out of our bedroom. "What is it, Sophie?"

"It's Eduard, Mama. He's alive, he's here to see me."

Mama just stared at me, her mouth open, her expression a mixture of surprise and alarm.

"Well, his family must be very happy."

"So am I, Mama."

"Then go and see him and let him know we are leaving tomorrow morning."

Willie was holding onto my long skirt. "Can I go with

you?"

"Nein, Willie, this is between Eduard and me."

With my heart racing, I stepped down the hall to the balcony, peeked over the railing into the lobby, and gasped. Eduard stood erect, his back to me, hands clasped behind him as he gazed at Papa's painting, *Cypress Cathedral.* He was taller and more muscular. He wore a white high collar shirt, a tan vest that accentuated his broad shoulders, matching trousers and black boots. Dashing! I looked down at myself, thankful that I had on a new pink and white dress. I pinched my cheeks for color and hurried down the stairs.

In the lobby I stopped, transfixed by the nearness of him after all these years. Marc Antony Eduard Meyer. He could be a Greek god, so tall and manly, with his blond hair that fell to his shoulders.

As I caught my breath, he seemed to sense my presence and turned to me. We were the only two people in the two-story room, and I ran to him. "Eduard!"

He opened his arms and wrapped them around me for the first time. I lay my head on his chest and wept. I could hear and feel his heart racing as tears ran down my cheeks.

"Sophie, you are even more beautiful than I remembered."

Then, just as Papa would have done, he reached in his pants' pocket and gave me a handkerchief. I wiped my tears away and looked up into his blue eyes. They were full of love but also a sadness that I had not seen before, no doubt from all the horrors of war.

"Oh Eduard, I feared you were never returning. Why did you take so long?"

"It's a long way to walk."

I gasped. "You walked the whole way?"

"Not the whole way. Occasionally I got a ride in a wagon."

"But you made it! You're like Odysseus."

He smiled. *"Ja,* because you sent me his words and I memorized them. They kept me going."

"Say the words, Eduard."

He lifted his chin and spoke in a rhythmic voice, almost singing.

"But, if so be that a God on the wine-dark
sea should o'erwhelm me,
That will I bear, for I hold an enduring
heart in my bosom:
For, ere this, have I toiled full much,
and much have I suffered
Both on the sea and in war: but come what
will, I can bear it."

He looked down at me then and, for a moment, we just gazed into each other's eyes, trying to believe that this was happening.

"Those words and thoughts of you kept me going, Sophie, and seeing you erases my suffering."

"And seeing you answers my prayers, Eduard, but ..." I shook my head sadly. "I'm sure you know that Papa was killed when a cannonball exploded near him."

"Ja, my mother told me. The sad news is all over Comfort. I grieve too because, in a way, he became like a father to me when we left for the war."

I nodded and tears came to my eyes again.

Eduard looked at me with his sad, loving eyes. "Sophie, your father loved you dearly and so do I, ever since that day in school when *Herr* Steves assigned us to read aloud from *William Tell,* me as Tell and you as my wife. It was prophetic, for I want to marry you someday when you're ready and I'm earning a living."

Something melted inside me, remembering that day, and I felt I might sink to the floor. But Eduard held me with his strong arms.

"May I kiss you?" he asked, just like the first time on Cypress Creek.

I lifted my chin and whispered, *"Ja."*

He leaned down, kissed my lips lightly, and straightened up again.

A thrill shot through my body, and I knew I did not want to part from him.

"Mama is taking us back to Germany tomorrow."

He shook his head. "I don't want you to go."

I stepped back, worried that someone could come in the lobby at any moment. Then I looked up and saw Willie peering over the second floor balcony.

"Choose us, Sophie," he said.

"Oh, Willie ..." My heart plunged. How could I ever leave him?

Eduard looked up at him. *"Guten Abend,* Willie."

"She's my sister," Willie shouted, ignoring his greeting. "She's going to Germany with us."

Eduard nodded and turned back to me with a question in his eyes.

Just then Mama came to the balcony railing. "Why, Eduard, you made it back! If only Friedrich ..."

"Ja, Frau Guenther, I mourn your husband. He treated me like his own son after we left Comfort."

"He wants Sophie to stay here," Willie told Mama.

"That's not possible, Eduard," Mama replied. "We leave tomorrow morning. It is what Friedrich wanted. Our passage is arranged."

It seemed that everyone else was deciding my fate, tossing me back and forth from one place to another.

"Do I not have something to say about where I live?"

Silence. A kind of silence that thunders in your head.

I remembered what Papa said in his letter: "Be true to yourself." So what was true? Leave Eduard, my love, never to meet again? Or leave my family, never to see them again? Never to see Willie grow up to be a man or Lena to become a woman? But especially Willie.

The silence expanded, filling the two-story space as we gazed from one to the other. Then I heard the front door open and some Confederate officers entered.

Mama said, "Come upstairs, Sophie, so we can discuss this in private."

"May Eduard join us?" I asked.

She hesitated. "I'm sorry you've traveled so far to no avail, Eduard, but you may join us for a moment to say farewell. Then we need to finish our packing."

As Eduard and I climbed the stairs, I did not know what to think or do. This was all so sudden. Decisions can change our lives forever. Should I leave my family or leave Eduard? How would Willie react if I decided to stay here? Would it ruin his life? And how would Eduard react if I decided to leave? Would he come with us?

My head began to throb. I rarely had headaches but now I did. I had to make a choice between two loves, and both meant change, a huge change that would rip my life in two. And I had to decide *now* which way to go.

Eduard and I entered the parlor. Willie took my hand, led me to the couch, and sat down beside me. Eduard sat on my other side. Mama and Lena were already sitting in the velvet upholstered chair by the window.

"So," Mama began, looking at me, "your father wants us to return to Dresden, and we owe it to him to obey his wishes."

"But Mama, he also said that if Eduard returned, I would have a difficult decision to make."

"I remember that Sophie but, as your mother, I think I have something to say in the matter." She glanced at Eduard, then back at me. "You cannot stay here alone. You're too young — you belong with family."

"But I have been accepted by Ursuline. The nuns would be my family."

"And after that ... what? Your future is uncertain."

Willie took hold of my hand. "Sophie, come with us."

I bit my lips together. My head throbbed. Whichever choice I made would hurt someone I loved.

"*Frau* Guenther," Eduard said, "may I tell you another wish of your husband's?"

Mama looked at him for a moment before answering. Then she nodded.

"We were bidding each other farewell before I was sent to the Army of Tennessee and did not know whether we would ever see each other again ... and indeed we did not." Eduard's face twisted and he paused to gain control of his emotions.

"He said, 'Eduard, do you love my Sophie?' I replied, '*Ja,* with all my heart and soul.' He smiled and said, 'Then promise me you will marry her if she is willing.' And I promised."

Oh, Papa, I thought, *you knew! If only you were here now, there would be no painful choice to make.*

Willie wrapped his arms around me. "Sophie, come with us," he repeated in a squeaky little voice and began to cry.

I patted his head as tears ran down my cheeks.

Silence. No one knew what to say, but I felt that Mama would never give in. Could I go against her will? Could I break Willie's heart?

"Why everybody crying?" Lena asked, looking up at Mama.

"Because, *Liebchen,* Sophie has to say farewell to Eduard."

I jumped up. *"Nein!* I'm going to make my own decision, Mama."

"Sophie, you are my daughter, still a child, and I will not allow you to stay here alone."

Eduard stood up beside me. *"Frau* Guenther, Sophie will not be alone. I am nineteen now and I swear to watch over your daughter, even as her father would have done."

Mama shook her head. *"Nein,* Eduard."

Then I had an idea. "Eduard, you once said you dreamed of attending architecture school in Leipzig. Why not come with us back to Germany?"

Eduard nodded. *"Ja,* that is so, but now that I have fought to keep this country whole, I want to be part of rebuilding it. And *Herr* Menger has offered to introduce me to an architect friend of his. He says there is much more opportunity here than in the old country."

That made sense to me.

"I am glad for you, Eduard," Mama said, "but Sophie will stay with us."

"Mama, you left your family for Papa and your future in Texas was uncertain," I reminded her.

"That is exactly why I am not letting you stay here."

"Mama, Eduard is the only man I will ever marry."

"You are too young to know your own heart at sixteen, Sophie."

"Then how did Juliet know Romeo was the only one for her?" My voice trembled.

"That is just a play."

"But based on a true story."

"That ended tragically."

I thought about that for a moment. Why did Juliet fail? Why did her story end tragically? And then I knew.

"Because she didn't stand up for what she wanted. Neither did Romeo. They both let others decide their fate. Now it's time for me to stand up and be true to myself. Time to decide my own fate. Papa always said, 'Everything that is alive grows and changes whether you want it to or not.'"

I paused, holding the next words in my heart, hoping I was making the right choice.

"And so I choose to stay in Texas. I've been accepted at Ursuline and I love Eduard. We both have a future here."

Eduard caught his breath. I turned and looked into his shining eyes and saw a promise of love and knew it was the right choice.

Mama frowned and held Lena close.

Willie clung to me. "No fighting!"

I looked down at him. "Willie, everything changes, like Papa said. He wants you to be brave and be the man of the family. Remember when he told you so?"

He sniffled and nodded.

"Now it is time for me to start my new life, just as one day it will be your time. It will tear my heart out to leave you and Mama and Lena, but it's not the end."

"What do you mean, Sophie?" Willie asked.

"I mean when you go back to Dresden, you can take art lessons and later go to the Academy of Fine Arts, just like Papa."

Willie jumped up and stood, hands on hips, and announced, "And I'll paint a portrait of you when you come to visit us."

My throat tightened and tears welled up in my eyes. "I would like that, Willie."

I turned to Mama. "Do you understand, Mama?"

She nodded slowly and a sad smile came to her face. "Well, I guess I've lost my daughter as well as my husband, but I still have Lena and my *Männlein.*"

"Not little, Mama," Willie protested.

A smile came to her face and she said, "*Nein,* not little."

"*Frau* Guenther, my dream is to visit Europe someday with Sophie, so I believe we shall all see each other again."

Suddenly I realized that my headache had all but gone away.

I looked down at Willie and tousled his blond curls. "So you see, *Liebchen,* it's not the end."

He looked up at me with a brave, man-of-the-family smile. "*Nein,* it's the beginning."

I smiled down at him. "Willie, you are wise beyond your years."

Thursday
July 12, 1865

Dear Reader,

But it *is* the end of this journal. There are only four pages left, and I need to tell about our farewell so I will never forget — though I scarcely know how I ever could.

We stood in a circle on the front gallery beside the bright red stagecoach, Eduard, the Mengers, Mama, Willie, Lena, and me. The early morning sun shone on the city market in Alamo Plaza, which was bustling with customers. Little did they know of our wrenching farewell. They knew only of choosing the perfect apple or asparagus stalk. I envied them.

All the baggage had been loaded into the boot at the rear of the stagecoach. The driver, the same burly man who brought us here months ago, settled his wide-brimmed hat on his head and put his hands on his hips.

"So, young man," he said to Willie, "you're gonna go back to Germany?"

Willie nodded with tears in his eyes.

"Well, son, don't you worry. We're gonna get you to the boat safe and sound."

Willie wiped his tears with the back of his hand, stood up straight, and tried to smile.

Young man indeed, dressed in his plaid shirt with a blue bow at his neck that matched his blue trousers and his eyes.

Mama stood beside me, wearing a paisley dress and straw bonnet that tied under her chin. She held Lena's hand.

Frau Menger hugged Mama. "As I told you, Elisabet, rest assured that we will take good care of Sophie until she goes to Ursuline ... and even after, if she needs us. I will be her Texas mother."

"Danke, Mary. You and *Herr* Menger have helped make our lives bearable during this awful time."

Herr Menger, ever the gentleman, smiled and nodded. "It was our pleasure, *meine Dame,*" my lady.

Suddenly Babette ran to Willie and hugged him. "I'll miss you, Willie."

He stood, arms at his side, not seeming to know what to do.

She stepped back and put her hands on her hips. "Will you miss me?"

He nodded. *"Ja,* you and your tricycle horse."

His childish, honest words brought a few chuckles amidst the tears.

Then Mama turned to me. "It's time, my Sophie."

A pang shot through my heart.

"Mama, I'll write to you. I have *Grossmutter*'s address."

"Ja, gut. And I will send letters to you at Ursuline."

I hesitated as we looked into each other's eyes. This was farewell to my childhood — no father and now no mother.

"I understand your decision, Sophie. Know, too, that I loved your father even as I hated Texas. And you, my first born child, will always live in my heart."

"We will we see each other again, won't we?" I asked, feeling hardness in my throat as tears brimmed in my eyes.

"If you come to Germany we will, but I will never set foot in Texas again."

We embraced for a moment.

Then she turned to Eduard who stood at my side. "I give my Sophie to you, Eduard, even as Friedrich did. Love her as did he."

"I will *Frau* Guenther and I do."

As she took her leave of the Mengers, I leaned down and hugged Lena.

"Be Mama's big girl," I said.

She nodded without a word as if she did not quite understand what was happening.

I stood and looked at Willie, who was watching me with sad eyes. I opened my arms and he ran to me, laid the side of his face on my chest, and reached his arms around my waist. We held onto each other for a moment and then I took him by the shoulders.

"Be strong, Willie, *meine Liebe.* Take care of Mama and Lena, and one day we will meet again."

He sniffed and wiped hard at his tears. "Promise?"

"I promise, and you know I always keep my promises."

He nodded.

"All aboard that's comin' aboard," the driver said.

I let go of Willie and took Eduard's hand as we watched my family board the stagecoach.

Willie leaned out the window. He had tears in his eyes but a little smile on his mouth.

The driver mounted his seat, slapped the reins on the horses' backs, and the stagecoach lurched ahead.

Willie waved until they rounded the corner.

Something wrenched inside my body and I covered my

face. Then I felt Eduard's arm around my shoulders. I looked up at him, so tall and stalwart. His face was thinner, more manly now. His golden hair shone in the sunlight. I saw the little scar above his eyebrow that I noticed when he first kissed me, there on Cypress Creek so long ago.

"You are my Odysseus, Eduard."

He looked down at me and smiled. "So that means you are my Penelope, and this is our new beginning."

Author's Note

This sequel has been in my mind ever since I finished *Sophie's War.* But somehow I could not imagine it until my friend and collaborator, Judy Ireson, came along. She is a former elementary school master teacher and principal.

I first met her at a Christmas bazaar book signing. She bought a copy of *Sophie's War,* telling me that it had been recommended along with one other book at Parnassus Books in Nashville, Tennessee. She bought the other one and now wanted *Sophie's War.*

Later, when Judy finished reading the book, she told me in detail what she loved about the story and ended with, "This book begs for a sequel!"

It was the word "begs" that spurred me on. As I outlined and then began writing, Judy and I often discussed the developing story, and she made valuable suggestions. If I got stuck, she pulled me out. I could not, would not have written this book without her.

Nor could I have written it without Cynthia Levinson and Shelley Jackson, who make up my small critique group. Both are professional authors of children's books, and Shelley is also an illustrator. They read every journal entry and wrote detailed comments on character development and story arc from a writer's point of view. They worried about Sophie, rejoiced when she succeeded, and cried when she grieved.

Thank you, ladies.

Writing a sequel is both easier and harder than writing the first book. Easier because I was already well acquainted with most of the characters and settings and had done much of the research, even though more would be needed. Harder because a sequel must stand alone. Not everyone who reads *Village Without Men* will have read *Sophie's War.* I had to find a way to bring a lot of information forward into the sequel without dumping it in the beginning. I had to sprinkle it throughout so as not to overwhelm readers and cause them to close the book.

Although Sophie's family is fictional, there are also real characters in this story.

Tante or Emma Altgelt wrote a brief memoir, which is preserved in manuscript form. I read and reread it many times. She really did teach Comfort children in her home after their teacher went to war. And she was something of a tomboy or *Wildfang,* who preferred riding out with her husband to round up their cows instead of cooking and caring for her children. Fortunately her mother took that role. Her husband, Ernst Altgelt, was indeed the founder of Comfort, Texas. In her memoir she called him "my dashing cavalier."

The Menger family is real and so is their hotel in San Antonio, which is still elegant and hospitable. During the Civil War guestrooms were closed except for a few to take in wounded soldiers, and the dining room served Confederate officers. I chose the Menger Hotel for Sophie and her family because my husband Tom and I loved it. We traveled there for special occasions like birthdays and anniversaries. And we always requested rooms in the oldest part of the hotel, on the second floor overlooking the patio, where Sophie stayed.

All the other places in the story are real. Comfort is still a small village of people proud of their German founders, and if not Freethinkers, still independent and unincorporated and basically unspoiled. I spent a lot of time there when I was writing *Sophie's War.* People welcomed me, including August Faltin, the great-grandson of one of the first settlers who operated Faltin Mercantile, where Sophie buys coffee and gets mail.

The historical background of the story is fact but not widely known. The German immigrants living in the Texas Hill Country during the Civil War were highly educated idealists who could not abide slavery. Nor did they want their country divided. It was a frightening time for them since Texas had seceded from the Union along with other southern states.

No matter what the Germans' beliefs, men were forced to join the Confederate Army or be dragged out of their homes, tortured, and hanged in front of their families, and their houses burned to the ground. To avoid this fate, many fled to Mexico and sailed to the North, like Papa and Eduard did, or back to Germany like *Herr* Altgelt.

Waldrip's Wolfpack was a real bunch of violent vigilantes who roamed the Hill Country looking for German Unionists and Confederate deserters. After the war Waldrip was indicted for murder and went into hiding near Fredericksburg. One day he ventured into town and was shot dead by a German resident. And so justice prevailed.

Now about the art: Before this book began I suffered the loss of my beloved Tom. We were not only partners in marriage but also in making books, he as illustrator and I as writer. Together we published many award-winning books. So how could I make one without his illustrations? The answer came from my son Karl and friend Judy. Karl painted Sophie's portrait for the cover, using tools of the 21st century to create a 19th-century image. Judy drew Papa's self-portrait and the house he planned to build after the war. I think Tom would be as proud as I am of the result.

This, then, is Sophie's journal, her words and thoughts, because as I entered her world, I left mine and became Sophie, experiencing her joys and sorrows. I shuddered as she witnessed the hanging, rejoiced when Pegasus was returned, wept when news of Papa's death arrived, and thrilled when Eduard finally appeared. I will miss being Sophie.

German Words

ach (ahkh)	alas
auf Wiedersehen (owf VEE-der-zayn)	goodbye
bitte (BIT-tuh)	please
Damen (DAH-men)	ladies
danke (DAHN-kuh)	thank you
Fachwerk (FAHKH-vehrk)	half-timber
Frau (frow)	Mrs.
Gott (gawt)	God
Grossmutter (GROSS-muh-ter)	Grandmother
gut, guter (goot, GOO-ter)	good
gute Nacht (GOO-tuh nahkht)	good night
guten Abend (GOO-ten AH-bend)	good evening
guten Morgen (GOO-ten MOR-gen)	good morning
Hängerbande (HAHNG-ger-bahnd)	hanging gang
Häuschen (HAUS-shen)	little (out)house
Häusfrau (HAUS-frow)	housewife
Herr (hehr)	Mr.
herzlich (HEHRZ-lickh)	heartfelt
Himmel (HIM-mehl)	heaven
ja (yah)	yes
Kinder (KIN-der)	children
kleine (KLINE-uh)	little
Liebchen (LEEB-chin)	little loved one
liebe (LEEB-uh)	love
Männlein (men-line)	little man
mein, meine (mine, MINE-uh)	my
nein (nine)	no
Tannenbaum (TAHN-nen-bowm)	fir tree

Tante (TAHN-tuh)	aunt
viel Glück (feel gluuk)	good luck
Weinachtsmann (VIGH-nahks-mahn)	Santa Claus
Wildfang (VILT-fahng)	tomboy
Willkommen (VIL-ko-men)	welcome
Zeitung (TSIGH-toong)	newspaper

Spanish Words

ahora (ah-OR-ah)	now
Alemán (ah-lay-MAHN)	German
tengo que ir (TENG-o kay ear)	I have to go
adios (ah-dee-OHS)	goodbye
muy bueno (MOO-ee BWEH-noh)	very good
todas (TOH-dahs)	all
las mujeres (lahs moo-HAIR-ehs)	the women
pistola (pis-TOL-ah)	pistol
niños (NEEN-yos)	children
guerra (GAIR-ah)	war
gracias (GRAH-see-us)	thanks
amigo (ah-MEE-go)	friend
si (see)	yes
paz (pahz)	peace
palabras (pah-LAH-brahs)	words

About the Author

Janice Shefelman says she became Sophie to write this journal. In her own life, Janice is an author with a strong interest in making the past come alive through historical fiction. Her books have won many awards, including the New York Public Library Best Book for Teens, the Children's Book Council Notable Book, Reading Rainbow Book, and the International Reading Association Children's Choices.

The love of books began when her father, a German professor at S.M.U. in Dallas, read to her from an early age, which led to careers as teacher, librarian, and writer. Books also gave her the desire to see the world. She spent one summer bicycling around Europe and another traveling in North Africa and the Middle East. When she married Tom, an architect, they set out on a yearlong trip around the world, traveling by freighter and living for a time in a Buddhist temple.

Her writing career began to blossom when her first book, *A Paradise Called Texas*, appeared on the Texas Bluebonnet Award Master List. Janice raised two sons with Tom and lives in Austin where she now devotes full time to writing.

For more please visit Shefelmanbooks.com

www.ingramcontent.com/pod-product-compliance
Lightning Source LLC
LaVergne TN
LVHW091146080826
845145LV00008B/2276

* 9 7 8 1 6 8 1 7 9 2 2 6 2 *